GILDEROY

This is a work of fiction. Names, characters, places and incidents either are the product of the author's imagination or are used fictitiously, and any resemblance to actual persons, living or dead, events. or locales is entirely coincidental.

ISBN: 978-0-6453770-5-7 (PB)
ISBN:978-0-6453770-6-4 (eBook)

Cover design by Clara Cassidy using Canva
Published by Jaymah
Torquay, Victoria, Australia

About the Author

Sage Quinn is a romantic at heart. She became captivated by stories of love after reconnection with her high school sweetheart after 40 years apart. When her family moved interstate - back before the days of the internet and social media - the pair lost touch. However, a freak reconnection via friends on social media brought them together again. Discovering their love hadn't died, they are now married and live on Victoria's Surf Coast. This is her debut novel.

Other Books by Jaymah

Judy Rankin
The Land of Giant Pineapples
Catalina
It's [Not] All About Liz!

Ivor Steven
Until Eyes Hear
Perception
Tullawalla

Bianca B
Neddy's Box of Noodles

John Wyndham
From Everywhere to Everywhere: The story of Sharing of Ministries Abroad

Website: www.jaymahpress.com.au
Email: info@jaymahpress.com.au
Ph: (+61) 0468 878 714

Sage Quinn

GILDEROY

Chapter One

Two men sat on what was once their paradise in the Yarra Valley. Surrounded by dense bushlands and open fields, waterways and walking tracks, expeditions were endless.

Charlie Dixon—the young go-to-man when a problem needed solving—sat staring without seeing. He turned his brooding face towards Pete 'Simmo' Simmons, his childhood best friend, but said nothing. What was there to say? Instead, he turned his gaze towards their dying campfire.

It had been years since they'd tracked through the bush to what they considered their special place. The place they swam, hunted, and escaped the outside world. Now, the outside world demanded attention as Charlie revisited the recent events that led to Simmo's return. And Simmo had come to stand by his mate as soon as he'd heard the news.

Charlie settled on a twisted, weathered log beside the campfire, mesmerised by the stifled glow flickering from orange to red as Simmo fed twigs and small branches into the glowing coals, coaxing them back to life. The ember's occasional crackle gave hope of resurrection. In the distance, the mechanical drone of a distinct reality broke through the serenity, yet Charlie seemed oblivious to the outside world waking. The dark silhouettes that enclosed the small campsite formed an all but blank canvas around him; dying stars above, flames licking the brewing pot and the smell of coffee entered his awareness. His rhythmic breathing slow and steady. Life continued—ready or not.

The dawn sun, still hidden behind the distant hills casting dark shadows on the oasis of cleared land through the bush, promised a day bright and warm as the waking birds began their morning chorus. Unseen in the trees, magpies warbled, cockatoos screeched and kookaburras laughed. Simmo and Charlie savoured a mug of strong, bitter coffee tamed with milk and sugar. The sky, tinged with muted orange, heralded the coming sun while the smoky smell of the summer campfire that, once upon a time promised warmth and comfort, now toyed with Charlie's senses and mind. The orchestra that played his favourite bush anthem seemed wasted.

Sitting opposite, Simmo watched for signs of engagement. The profile of his mate's expertly cropped hair and rugged facial features were hard to distinguish as he blended well with his dense surroundings. Charlie's long legs forced his knees high as he sat, broad shoulders slumped forward, with arms resting on legs. He looked like a broken man.

Charlie and Simmo had grown up on the edge of the wide-open spaces of farming lands and vineyards of The Valley. Their hometown, a little removed from the open valley, nestled in the still thick timbered forest and bushlands. As boys, they'd done everything together in the small community: played Aussie Rules for the local team, joined the Country Fire Authority as volunteers, and planned many adventures. They regularly 'went bush' in their teens, camping and trekking, feeling more at home sleeping under the stars and wrestling nature than being cooped up and moulded into society's routine. Being two of only a handful of eligible young men in the town with a population of 300, they embraced the mantles of local heartthrobs chasing the girls and sporting heroes. While Pete Simmons had moved the hour or so away to suburbia for work as a junior lawyer, Charlie couldn't imagine living elsewhere.

Charlie's lifelong dream was simple: to own land and lead a self-sufficient life with his dream woman. Unlike Simmo, the ambitions of a corporate career, which had been on offer after university, had never been his. His few years at uni, away from The Valley gave him adequate exposure to city life and convinced him it was not for him.

Charlie and Simmo had drifted apart after uni. Over time, their circle of friends changed, activities altered. However, they were still always there for each other when it counted–celebrating milestone birthdays, engagements, deaths, and grand finals. And, while Simmo preferred the city life, he could still enjoy the occasional trip back to his bush roots.

Charlie met Myra Bennett in his final year at university. The gregarious, exciting young woman was almost the opposite of Charlie. While he studied agriculture, Myra studied business and their paths rarely crossed. Little did either know, they lived within 200 metres of each other for the best part of three years.

Their paths finally crossed on a back road of The Valley when, stuck at the side of the road with a flat tyre and no car jack, Charlie came to Myra's aid. Home for the weekend to play for the Demons in the footy grand final, he noticed a young woman waving wildly next to a car parked by the side of the road. Dressed in designer jeans, shirt and now muddied high-heeled stiletto shoes, he thought she looked comical standing beside her vehicle. The young woman, with golden locks cut short, heavy eye makeup and lips painted in a vibrant hue–clearly from the city–needed rescuing. He couldn't help but wonder what she was doing on this road few tourists took.

“No jack in your car?” asked Charlie.

"Whether I have a jack or not, I still wouldn't be changing this tyre. I'd be calling roadside assistance.” A cheeky grin crossed her face. “I didn't expect no phone coverage out here.”

Charlie was intrigued by the mischievous twinkle in her eyes and eager to assist the attractive stranger who appeared forlorn but by no means helpless.

"I'm Charlie," he said, held out his hand.

"Myra." She clasped his hand, shaking it with confidence.

"So, what are you doing out here in The Valley without a car jack?" Charlie asked as he moved to the back of his truck and retrieved the needed tools.

"To be honest, I don't quite know. Felt like a drive in the country?"

"Are you on your way to the country?" he asked, with a grin. "Or on your way home?"

"On my way home," she grinned, noting the mockery of his question.

"It's beautiful out here. A great place to clear your head," she said, thinking back to a different time and place.

Charlie noticed a troubled look fleetingly cross her face before she moved and crouched beside him, picking up the spanner and holding it towards Charlie.

"What are you doing?" he asked.

"Helping."

"Helping? Thanks, but I'll be fine. Go sit under that tree over there. Enjoy the country and ... clear your head. This won't take long."

Turning to look, Myra noted the closeness of the trees, the dark shadows and thick vegetation. "No, no, no! I'm not going to sit on the ground. Who knows what's in that tree or in the long grass? Besides, it'll be quicker if I help."

Charlie smiled. "You're not from around here, are you?"

Myra giggled. "That obvious, huh?"

Still holding the spanner, she stood and looked around. The thick bush quickened the fading light. "It's just so quiet."

Charlie stood beside her, silence filling the air between them briefly. "Yep. It's a great place. Pretty special out here."

"You live locally?" she asked.

"Yeah, about ten minutes in that direction," he replied, pointing to an adjoining road.

"Are you a farmer?"

Charlie laughed, "Not quite. I grew up in Gilderoy. Mum and Dad still live there. I live in Coburg while at uni. But I hope to return to Gilderoy, or the district, when I finish at the end of the year."

"Oh! I'm at uni, too. Which one are you at?" Myra asked excitedly.

"RMIT."

Me too!" she replied, rather animated. "What are you studying?"

"Environmental science. Doing my honours year. I'm a farmer at heart, but I want to learn new ways of doing things. You know, better for the environment, more productive ..."

"Wow! That's awesome. Updating farming techniques can contribute to environmental conservation. I think all farmers should study the environment. We only have one planet and they need to stop killing it with pesticides." Myra was in her element. One of the many causes she felt passionate about.

"You sound like a greenie. Ever spent time out on a farm? Or is your knowledge all gained from books and living in the city?" Charlie replied, annoyed that yet another city slicker was making a judgment on something they knew little about.

"I'm sorry. I don't mean to sound critical, but—"

"It's okay. Come spend a bit more than a day in the country, get to know some farmers, and then you can jump on your soapbox if you want."

Charlie went back to changing the tyre. His initial impression that Myra was intriguing had waned. Although beautiful—in a city girl kind of way—she seemed just like all the other city folks who lived in a bubble of misinformation.

Myra didn't understand how but knew she'd offended Charlie. She was disappointed. She didn't want to upset her rescuer. Taking a step backwards, she gave him space to get on with the job.

As Charlie tightened the nuts, the muscles in his broad shoulders and arms clenched. The tone of his arms excited her. She liked the look of her personal roadside assistant.

Charlie glanced in Myra's direction. She stood biting her lip and smiling. Her eyes looked ravenous as she scanned his body. Charlie frowned choosing to ignore her and returned his attention to the tyre.

With the tyre changed, he let go of the slightly offensive remarks she'd made, deciding not to let the opinions of someone he'd never see again spoil his day.

"All done," he exclaimed, as he packed up the tools.

"Thank you. Can I just check, if I continue on this road, will it lead back to the highway?" Myra asked sheepishly.

Charlie grinned. "Yeah, straight up for about 2 ks and you'll hit the road to Gilderoy and onto the highway. You'll see the signs."

Myra bowed, hands together, and uttered, "Namaste," before getting in her car. She waved her arm out the window as she drove away.

Charlie frowned, confused by the greeting, but waved back. Walking towards his truck, he shook his head. That was different.

Several weeks elapsed before their paths crossed again while crossing Swanston Street outside RMIT. Myra concentrated on a text message while Charlie studied a map. Their bodies collided.

"Oh! Sorry, I wasn't looking where I was ... Charlie?"

"Yeah. Hi. Sorry ..." Charlie looked confused.

"Myra," she stated as if he should have known.

Charlie stood frowning as Myra waited, confident he would make the connection.

His face lit up. "Myra! Right. How's the tyre going? Staying inflated?"

"Yes, thank you," she laughed.

They stood uncomfortably, smiling at each other. Myra took one last look at her phone before putting it away.

"Ah... um..." she pointed at the map in Charlie's hand. Words failed her.

As if suddenly realising he had something in his hands, Charlie stammered, "Oh! Ah...I'm just on my way to see someone in building 91, but I have no idea where that is."

"I think that's over on Victoria Street, isn't it?" Myra offered.

"Augh! Why is RMIT so spread out? I'm going to be late and this guy can be pedantic. He's just as likely to tell me I'm too late and must reschedule."

"This guy?" Myra asked. "Sorry, none of my–" She stopped. She didn't need to know.

Charlie could feel his face warming under the blush he knew would take over his cheeks.

"A professor," he blurted, holding the paper in his hands out for Myra to see.

She scanned the map before grabbing Charlie by the hand. "Come on, I'll show you the way," she said as they charged off in the opposite direction.

That was the start of their sometimes-tumultuous relationship. He was a simple man with simple needs. She was the city girl.

Chapter Two

Charlie sat ashen faced, nursing injured limbs, staring at the still smouldering remains that had been home. All the hard work renovating the run-down old cottage, his whole life was in the blackened embers that lay before him—the life he and Myra had begun just a year earlier.

He tried calling Myra to tell her about the fire, but she wasn't answering.

Where was she?

Charlie looked at the ruin before him. All was destroyed.

He was kicking himself for their silly dispute about holiday destinations. Arguments had become a standard way for the two to communicate. She'd state her case, he'd counter it, and the pendulum would swing from one to the other until eventually Charlie backed down and Myra called it a compromise. But not this time. This time, he'd walked out, leaving everything unresolved. She was most likely not answering her phone because she was still pissed off with him.

Surveying the rubble that had been their home, the choice between a resort in Queensland and a tent in the outback became pointless. He had accused her of selfishness, narrow-mindedness, pigheadedness and for what?

They had bought and renovated the old house on the flats between the main road to Powelltown and the Little Yarra River. Gilderoy, once a thriving saw-milling town surrounded by large native trees perfect for timber milling, today was now little more than a quaint, sleepy hollow with a few homes and a decreasing population.

Myra and Charlie had only used timber grown and harvested in The Valley, in keeping with its rustic charm and Myra's environmental beliefs steeped in city book knowledge. They had expanded the little cottage and constructed it solely with the help of the local people.

Charlie now sat in a giddy haze as the authorities rummaged through the ashes and he struggled to make sense of what he saw before him.

"Sarg, can you come here?" called the fire officer.

"What is it, Mac? Find something useful?" asked police sergeant Phil Cook.

"Not so much something, but ... someone." He said quietly, turning away from Charlie.

"Where? In the rubble?" Phil Cook asked in disbelief.

"Yeah, if I'm not mistaken, I'd say these are small human bones."

"Ah, shit! Any idea what room this was?"

Mac looked around as he tried to decipher the house layout. "The lounge. If I remember correctly, the old fireplace in the lounge backed onto part of the kitchen. Mind you, I haven't been in the house since they started the renos."

"Okay."

"Sarg," he paused as he moved and pointed to another pile of ashes. "Look over there. Is that ...

"More bones," finished the sergeant.

The bones, blackened by fire and ripped clean of any flesh, protruded under the smoking remains that had once been a house.

"Okay, boys, let's get the tape up and keep everyone back."

As Charlie watched the group of men, a feeling of icy dread came over him. He couldn't hear, but the other men's awkward movements and turned heads suggesting something sinister. This was more than just his home being engulfed in flames.

"Charlie, you got onto Myra yet?" yelled the police sergeant, moving towards him.

"No, the phone is switched off. She's probably at her mother's. Phone coverage isn't great there."

"Want to try the landline? To make sure."

"I saw you looking at something. What have you found?"

Phil Cook, not looking at Charie, shuffled and sighed as he replied, "There's no easy way to say this, Charlie. There's bones."

Charlie's blank face drained of colour. His breathing became more audible as his small, strangled voice cried out, "No. No! No!" Charlie attempted to stand, but the injuries to his limbs saw him slip and fall, unable to get a footing. He reached for Phil to drag himself up before collapsing.

"Calm down, Charlie. We don't know anything yet. But ... they look human."

"No! If she were gone, I'd know! I'd feel it! You're mistaken..." He cried out before crumbling to the ground. The ground blurred and seemed to spin uncontrollably. Voices, sounds, images all distorted. Nothing made sense. As Charlie struggled to breathe and grasp what was being suggested, he lay back so he could no longer see the carnage.

The sky, so blue. So perfect. This can't be happening, he thought.

An ambulance arrived. Paramedics promptly assessed and sedated Charlie as he thrashed around the ground, crying, punching the earth, oblivious to his surroundings. Darkness and a tormented peace descended, one that may never recognise beautiful, blue, clear skies again.

¥

After their second meeting on Swanston Street, Charlie had investigated where Myra's lecture rooms were and planned the accidental crossing of paths on more than one occasion. Each time, he'd claim the country boy in the city got lost easily and needed Myra to come to his rescue.

All the while, Myra, who could see through his ploy, wondered why he didn't just ask her out. Out of desperation, she eventually initiated the first date to put the poor boy out of his misery. The romance between

Charlie and Myra then took off like a rocket. Unless they had lectures or work to attend, they were inseparable.

Everything progressed with ease until Charlie graduated six months before Myra. He had intended to return to The Valley and take up a position with the State Environmental Department. Myra had been supportive of this over the year they'd been seeing each other, but she wasn't happy now that Charlie was leaving her in the city to finish her degree. Charlie didn't want to leave her either but maintained it would only be for a short period.

Charlie, wanting Myra to join him, argued that many businesses–of all sizes–needed managers in The Valley. She could gain business experience there. He also hoped it would give her time to fall in love with the rural setting and never want to leave.

Myra could see the merit in his argument, but also hoped it would give her time to coax Charlie out of the country and back to her real world in the city.

Eventually, they found a compromise. Charlie would move to Gilderoy and take up his new position and Myra would join him once she had graduated and they'd work the rest out later. One step at a time, they agreed.,

Myra had barely settled into her new country home when she and Charlie exchanged vows. They bought a ten-acre block of land with an old two-bedroom wooden shack. Myra refused to give up on the old, character-filled shack, renovating and expanding it with a modern extension that perfectly blended the old and new. She justified it as a metaphor for their relationship. They had chosen each other for better or worse, even though it would never be easy.

Charlie and Myra lived in the old shack during renovations, shifting rooms as needed. The shack was nearly complete when Isabella became part of their little family.

Baby Isabella had been a surprise, but not an unpleasant one. She was the last component of Charlie's life plan. He now had it all. The woman and home of his dreams and their first child. Myra was happy for Charlie. While she loved her life and family, she couldn't help but feel something was missing. This life wasn't quite what she had planned, but it was enough for now.

¥

With burns on his arms, hands and feet, and in severe shock, Charlie had been taken to the local hospital for observation. For five days, he struggled with reality. Heavily sedated, in his lucid moments, Charlie struggled to find the words to explain or come to terms with what had happened.

In his subdued state, he dreamt of Myra, the petty argument, his dismissal of her idea of a holiday. He heard the baby cry but couldn't comfort her.

Charlie thrashed about, trying to escape the imagery as he dreamt those final moments. Myra wasn't listening to him anymore. Negotiation had never been her strong point, but since the baby's arrival, she'd seemed more self-centred than ever. Sitting on a beach in northern Queensland, sun baking for a week while someone else looked after their child was not his idea of a holiday. He refused to back down this time.

"Charlie, don't do this," came the plea.

"What sort of holiday is that? It's our first family trip, My!"

"Charlie, the baby. Think of the baby."

"I am thinking of the baby!"

"And what about me?"

His vision blurred as smoke filled the room.

A scream.

The baby crying.

The smell was overpowering.

"Breathe. I can't breathe."

"Charlie, I'm sorry..."

Charlie felt trapped and couldn't wake up from the nightmare.

Why had he been so pigheaded?

¥

Charlie lay looking around the white room he found himself in, attempting to make sense of the recurring dream. It wasn't real, he told himself. He wasn't in the house when the fire started.

His thoughts turned to beautiful Issie G. So tiny, helpless, vulnerable, beautiful. He would have done anything for her, so why couldn't he save her?

Think of the baby. Myra often used the baby in her arguments, as she knew it left him defenceless.

"Isabella," he whispered as if calling her to him.

Disbelief filled him, thinking that he may never see those pale brown eyes and her dimpled smile again was too much to comprehend. The pain. His heart was being wrenched from his chest.

Charlie turned, struggling to get away from his cloudy thoughts. He tried to focus the small room around him. On one side, a small window with bars on the outside let filtered sunlight through the blinds. On the other, a light-toned wooden door shut the room. Machines whirred near his head as he noticed a beeping noise. Looking down, he noted the intravenous drip attached to the back of his right hand.

"Mr. Dixon, you're awake. I'm Dr. McMahon. How are you feeling?"

Charlie looked at the man he'd failed to see standing by the machine. He hazily remembered being asked that question on several occasions, but, as with previous times, it seemed a question he could not answer. He seemed only capable of silence.

"Do you know where you are?"

Charlie didn't reply. He tried, but no words came out.

"You're in The Valley District Hospital. You've been here for five days. Sergeant Cook is outside. He would like to talk to you, but only if you feel up to it. What do you think?"

The room continued to wobble as Charlie again tried to focus his attention. He couldn't believe he'd been there for five days, as the doctor claimed. He searched his memory and recalled a strange voice, a small prick, and pressure on his arm.

"Charlie, I'm going to let the Sergeant in. You don't have to say anything if you don't want to. They just want to talk to you. Okay?"

The clean-pressed clinical doctor moved toward the door without waiting for Charlie's reply.

Charlie knew of Dr. McMahon but more by reputation. He was known to have a poor bedside manner, as Charlie could now attest. But, he was meant to be a good doctor. Charlie held off his final judgment.

As Charlie watched the doctor move through the once-closed door, he glimpsed the police sergeant at the entry.

"He's conscious but still not speaking. You can try talking with him, but don't be surprised if he says nothing." Charlie heard Dr. McMahon as he left the room.

"I'll be here if you need me." A comment meant for Charlie as much as for the police sergeant.

"Charlie. How are you?" began the sergeant, as he walked slowly towards Charlie.

Sergeant Cook and Charlie Dixon were well-known to each other. He was the man who had picked up the drunk Charlie and Simmo at the side of the road as underage teenagers. *"I won't tell your folks this time, you two. But if I see you like this again ..."*

The same man had shut down the main street of Gilderoy on Charlie and Myra's wedding day.

"I'm sorry, but there's a big tree blocking the road. You can't get through this way. You'll have to go a different way. Yes, I know it's inconvenient, but there's nothing

I can do about it," he said to drivers out for a day trip.

The Gildie Pub wasn't big enough for the gathering of people celebrating the marriage of two much-loved young people. The celebrations spilled out onto the street as band, impromptu bar and dancing took over the small town.

Now, Sergeant Cook approached. The look in his eyes told Charlie the man wasn't here for friendly banter. His posture and walk appeared formal, yet his eyes gave him away and a sadness filled the void between the two men.

Charlie croaked, "Where's Myra and Issie? What's happening?" The look on Sergeant Cook's face released a painful memory in Charlie's mind. "The fire. You found ... something ..."

"I'm sorry, Charlie. There were two bodies found in the fire. They were badly burned and little more than bones. We believe them to be the remains of little Isabella and Myra." As the sergeant fought to remain in control, it was impossible for him not to crack as the horror came crashing in on Charlie once again.

The room spun out of control and filled with shadows as Charlie puked on the bed. The small amount of bile, liquid and mucus left his body as the realisation tried to sink in. The police sergeant took a step back as the doctor and a nurse appeared to again sedate the troubled man.

"No," Charlie protested as he headed toward an uncontrollable limbo world. The room spun and voices became distant, causing his mind to fog over. He battled to hold on to reality, but it was in vain. The fog engulfed him.

"I suggest you go for now, Sergeant and let him rest."

Charlie heard the echoing voice.

"Charlie, we need to speak with you about the fire. I'll come back. Take it easy, mate. We'll work through this."

The days passed filled with nightmares of raging flames, crying babies, Myra screaming and a feeling of powerlessness as Charlie battled the imaginings of what he was told; this was more than a nightmare. The harsh reality overwhelmed him, and he struggled to grasp it, feeling his sanity slipping away.

He returned to consciousness as the nurse came for her morning rounds.

"No more sedatives. I can't think. I can't escape the nightmare. I need to wake up. No more," he pleaded.

"Charlie, you've had a terrible shock. It would be best if you stayed calm," she asserted. "I'll talk to the doctor for you."

Charlie slept again. The nightmares eased and darkness outside greeted him as he woke. He could see through the door to his room, open just a crack, to what he thought was a police uniform in the hallway. He buzzed for a nurse.

"Can I have water?"

The nurse was young and her hands shook as she poured the water and assisted him to drink.

"Is that a cop out there?"

"Umm, yes," the nervous nurse responded.

"Why's he there?"

"Just rest, Mr. Dixon. The doctor will be around to see you in the morning." The nurse replaced the cup on the chest of drawers with trembling hands.

Charlie's mind felt vague as questions tried to form. If only he could remember what had been real and what he had imagined over the last ... how many days had it been? He didn't know as, again, he drifted to sleep.

Images, stretched and distorted, filled his mind.

"Do you, Charles Dixon, take Myra Janine Bennett as your lawfully wedded wife?"

"I do."

"Do you, Myra Janine Bennett, take Charles Dixon as your lawfully wedded husband?"

"I…"

"Myra?"

"I…guess I do. Sorry, yes, I do."

Caught in the memory, Charlie remembered the happiest day of his life and how he refused to let her hesitation overshadow it.

Charlie tossed in his sleep.

At the reception, Myra explained her hesitation as nerves. He hadn't doubted her, but now, in his groggy state, it sat disturbingly.

"Myra," he called.

They had been happy, hadn't they? Charlie felt trapped. Where was she? She couldn't be gone.

If only he could clear his mind.

Chapter Three

"Charlie, you coming?" yelled Reedy from the truck.

"Hang on, mate. Myra?" He looked at his wife, waiting for her permission.

"Charlie, I'm tired. The baby needs changing. Can we just go home?"

"I won't be long, I promise. An hour tops."

"We need to make a decision about this trip!"

"The sooner we get the school cleaned up, the better for the kids. We can talk when I get back."

"Whatever. Go. We both know you're going to. I'm too tired to argue with you."

¥

Charlie stirred. Why hadn't he gone home with her?

He had overheard Marjory talking to Myra as he'd headed out of the store.

"Must be hard living with a town hero," queried Marjory, sweeping the aisle a few metres away.

"You have no idea. It's like he's oblivious to me. There's always a 'higher' or 'more important' cause to be dealt with."

"He'd want to be careful. He might come home one night to find it empty," Marjory hinted.

"No, it's okay," replied Myra, shoulders slumping, "I knew what I was marrying. His generous spirit is one thing I fell in love with."

"We all have our limits, darl."

Myra turned and locked eyes with Charlie, who smiled and blew a kiss.

¥

Charlie woke with a start. He should have gone home, he thought. The dull feeling in his head made it feel heavy. He couldn't think straight; couldn't escape the torment.

Raising himself with bandaged hands, he sluggishly moved his legs over the edge of the bed. His gaze fell on his covered feet momentarily before returning to his thoughts. He had to find Myra. He had to find his daughter. They couldn't have been in the fire; they just couldn't, he thought. It was incomprehensible.

The room swayed as Charlie pulled the drip out from the back of his hand. A stinging pain shot up his arm as blood trickled from the wound. The intermittent beeping accompanying his room became a constant tone as he removed the medical shackles to stand. His bandaged legs were weak and wouldn't take his weight as he stumbled and fell, pushing the noisy machine away. He lay on the cool floor, energy expended, and looked at the crepe covering on one hand.

The door to the room opened as the nurse he'd seen earlier in the night entered, along with the policeman who sat outside the room. They rushed to his side, helping him up from the floor and moving him back towards the bed. But Charlie didn't want their help. As he protested, the officer overpowered him. Charlie, extremely weak, unwillingly submitted.

"I just want to find my family!" he pleaded.

"Mr. Dixon, please. I've called the doctor. Just wait," the nurse instructed, backing away.

Charlie looked at the young woman, surprised to see fear in her eyes. "What's wrong?" he growled, annoyed at the situation. "You look scared– augh, if only my head weren't so fuzzy!"

Charlie held his head, wishing with all his might for the fog to clear.

"Okay, Mr. Dixon, sit still. The doc is on his way. Let's just remain calm." The constable with untidy hair and stubbly chin spoke with authority and compassion as. Had the man had been sleeping outside his room?

Nothing made sense as they waited for the doctor. The nurse busied herself tidying the scattered bed linen and skewed medical machines.

Charlie wondered if he was still sleeping. His throbbing injured feet suggested this was not a dream.

The nurse turned the machine off, killing the high pitched done that had filled the room leaving just the ticking clock to break the quiet in the all-but-silent room. The only other sound was the nurse tapping on a keyboard by the hospital computer system. Now and then, Charlie would see her steal a weary glimpse at him as he stared at the vinyl tiles on the floor, following their grey and cream checkered pattern to the wall. He systematically counted the squares from one wall to the next and breathed evenly to regain control of his mind, vision, and the room.

Through the curtained window, the day began with a dull light. As if reading his mind, the nurse moved to the window to open the blinds and let the light in. Outside, a grey mist masked the day. The outline of the tops of trees could be made out, but not much more.

While looking at the window, Charlie saw a glimpse of his reflection. A shadow hung over his thinner frame. Charlie's face appeared drawn, and his usual stubble looked long. Myra wouldn't be happy and would ask him to shave it back as soon as she saw it, he thought.

He was lost in a hospital haze when the door opened and his thoughts returned to the room. A tall, stocky man with slicked-back sandy-coloured hair walked to the computer monitor. The doctor looked over at Charlie and smiled before returning to the monitor. He wasn't the man Charlie remembered seeing earlier.

"Thank you, constable. I'm sure we don't need your presence at the moment," Dr Silvers dismissively pronounced, barely turning to address at the officer and continuing to look at the monitor. He soon moved to the foot of the bed and spoke to the nurse. "You're free to go too if you'd rather."

The young nurse didn't need to be told twice. She scurried away following the sergeant as quickly as possible. Charlie watched on.

"Mr. Dixon. How are you feeling? I'm Dr. Silvers, a psychiatrist here at The Valley Hospital. I've just been reading your notes. Sounds like you've had an interesting time of late."

"Where is Dr McMahon?"

"He's asked me to come in and have a chat."

"Oh? Why?"

"It seems you've taken the news of your wife's death hard and- “

"She's not dead."

Dr Silvers paused. "Can you tell me where she is then?"

"I don't know, but she's not dead."

"I see," Dr Silvers said, hesitating a moment.

"Mr. Dixon, what can you tell me about the last two weeks?"

Charlie felt a slap in the face. Two weeks, surely not.

"I can't tell you much, doctor. I've been drugged for I don't know how long."

"You've been sedated."

"I don't want to be sedated anymore. I want to know what's going on."

"Do you remember the fire, Mr. Dixon?"

"Yes. I've had vivid dreams thanks to the drugs they've been pumping into my system. It has to stop! I can't think straight. I don't know what's real—what's not. Please, tell them to stop sedating me!"

"It does look like they have been a little heavy-handed with the medication. I'll talk to Dr. McMahon. You had some nasty burns, Mr. Dixon. Your body needs time to heal."

"How is sending me senseless 'good for me'?"

"You were injured in the fire, Mr. Dixon. Your body went into shock. And, according to the reports here, you had moments of violence. The doctor was concerned for your safety and that of his staff."

"Okay, stop. I don't know what you're talking about. My memory of the last ... however long, is sketchy. Can we start at the beginning, please?" Charlie's exasperation at the riddles and innuendo grew. No one was giving him answers, just more questions.

"Your home has been destroyed by fire. There's nothing left. It would appear there was some kind of explosion, but the investigation is continuing. When the fire brigade arrived, you were frantically attempting to put the flames out with your bare hands and feet. When the authorities found bodies in the ashes, you became hysterical. During sedation, you spoke to your wife and apologized. Do you remember any of this?"

"I told you; I've been forced to live in a haze. I hardly know who I am, let alone what I've supposedly said!"

"Okay. Try to stay calm."

Sergeant Cook appeared and knocked on the door.

"My constable informed me you were here. Can I come in?" he asked.

Not waiting for a reply, the sergeant entered the room, giving Charlie a diluted smile. He introduced himself to the psychiatrist.

Dr Silvers beeper sounded. Charlie sighed with relief as Dr. Silvers excused himself, promising to return. Maybe now he could get some answers, he thought.

Cookie told of the events thus far, but reminded Charlie that the investigation wasn't over. It appeared the fire had started when the Dixon's car hit the house with some force. Due to the intensity of the explosion, they inspected the gas line for a rupture. It appears the driver of the car had been thrown through the front windscreen before the vehicle exploded into flames that engulfed the house. It was only a matter of minutes before it became unsalvageable. The house was fully alight when a passing car noticed the smoke and flames and alerted the fire brigade.

As the sergeant spoke, Charlie sat staring at the checkered floor tiles, fighting to hold on to something that made sense. The room swayed, but he refused to give in to his body. He needed to hear the details. He needed to make sense of what was happening.

"And the ... the bodies?" Charlie asked.

"I'm sorry, Charlie," replied the sergeant.

Charlie looked up and shook his head. "No. I don't believe it. If they were gone, I'd know. I'd feel it! You've made a mistake. Something's ... something's not right."

Charlie's breath was deep and forceful as he grappled with the news. They weren't gone. They couldn't be.

"Charlie, I have some tough questions I need to ask you."

"Ask," said Charlie, not taking his eyes from the floor.

"Where were you when the fire broke out?"

Charlie turned to face his friend.

"What? You know where I was. Why are you asking me, Cookie?"

"I have to ask, Charlie."

"I was at the school, helping clean up after the storm!"

"Did you know Myra was at home?"

Charlie sighed. "I remember leaving her in town. She was going home and wanted me to go with her. But..."

"Were you having financial problems, Charlie?"

"Financial problems? Things were tight, but we were okay." Charlie didn't make the connection of what was being implied straight away. "Why do you ask?"

"The house was insured for more than it was worth, wasn't it, Charlie?"

The penny dropped. "So, you think I set fire to my own house? Come on, Cookie, you know me better than that."

"Mr. Dixon." Charlie suddenly realised Dr McMahon was beside him, checking his blood pressure. He hadn't seen or heard the man enter the room. "I know this is difficult for you. Would you like to stop for a while?"

"No! I want to know all. Is this why there's been a constable outside my room for days? Do you think I had something to do with destroying my home and family? This is ridiculous!"

"No, Charlie. It's routine questioning. You know that. And I thought it'd be better coming from me than someone else."

Charlie sat staring at the stark white room with the checkered floor, seeming unable to understand what he was hearing. He'd lost everything. The old cottage he'd slaved over to create a haven for his family. His wife and daughter, apparently. All gone! He'd given everything he had to help Myra feel comfortable in the bush—the least was building her the house she wanted. What the police officer, his friend, suggested was ludicrous. He didn't care about the financial loss. That was nothing compared to the loss of his family.

Charlie crawled down under the stark white covers on the hospital bed. With his back to the men, he lay there attempting to make sense of the situation. He hoped to awaken and discover it had been a dream. Was he still hallucinating from the sedatives he'd been on? *Wake up. Wake Up, Charlie!*

But there was no waking up from this nightmare.

Chapter Four

The sun stood over the hill as Charlie and Pete relived their youth. Somewhere in the bush was their favourite swimming hole. Neither had been there for years and wondered if they'd remember the way. The track they had created through the large gum trees and scrubby underbrush many years ago had all but disappeared.

With the campfire doused just after 10 am, backpacks were loaded with drinking water, towels and sunscreen—a little more than they would have thought about when they were boys.

"We're showing our age, mate," laughed Pete. "Back in the day, it would have been a few stolen beers from your dad's fridge, and no water or sunscreen."

He guffaws a little too loudly.

"Don't remember even packing a towel," replied Charlie soberly.

"Nah, ten minutes laid out on the hot rocks was all the drying we needed back then."

"Lots changed in the last fifteen years." said a wistful Charlie.

"Hey, come on, mate. Hang in there."

Pete gave Charlie a little shake and warm smile. The melancholy left Charlie's face as the two finished preparations, ready to set off.

In the shade of the tall trees, the distant hum of the city disappeared. Sunlight cast dappled shadows through the trees, on the world below the canopy. Lizards, bathing in the sun, scampered as the men approached. Like a waving sea of green, fern fronds laid-out before them as the men wandered, looking for once familiar signs indicating they were heading in the right direction.

They walked in near silence for the best part of an hour before the trees and scrub parted, exposing a watering hole. A long, grey, sandy shore sharply fell away to the edge of the water held in a kidney-shaped basin. Scarcely thirty feet long and twenty feet wide, the men stood quietly surveying the oasis. Dark and still, it stood before them. The river that once fed the pool lay dry and empty.

"I remember it as bigger than this," said Charlie.

"And I don't remember so much sand," replied Pete. "Where's the river gone? Ok, it was never much of a river, more a creek, but this is pathetic."

"Still want to swim?"

"Not a chance!"

"I wasn't that keen before we started," Charlie said, sitting on a boulder by the trees. He was tired. The doctor had said it might take a week or more before the effects of the sedatives disappeared from his system and warned not to overdo physical activities for a while. Following the doctor's orders wasn't a problem as he hadn't wanted to do anything since leaving the hospital a few days before.

Pete slumped on a boulder next to him. He'd hoped a trip down memory lane would be a positive experience for Charlie and help bring him out of the sadness that had all but swallowed him. Despite the doctor's advice against physical activity, Pete felt it was precisely what his friend needed. Now, as they sat on the boulders with the dismal excuse of a swimming hole before them and the shallow, sunken look on his friend's face, he wished he hadn't.

"I'm sorry, mate," Pete said.

"For what?"

"I thought you might enjoy–"

"Don't. 'Enjoy' is not a word I want to hear. It's not part of my life anymore."

No words could provide comfort. No one had the power to change the torment Charlie endured. Pete watched him go through the days without reason or desire for an outcome. Too many questions remained unanswered. Charlie's life had become surreal with the storm, argument with Myra, and loss. Pete wished for it to be an illusion and for his friend to return.

A phone rang—the sound echoing around the trees.

"You going to answer that?" asked Pete.

"Why? They can leave a message," Charlie replied despondently.

"Give it here," Pete said, reaching forward.

Charlie dutifully did as he was told, reaching into his pocket and passing the phone over.

"Hello?" Pete said, answering the ring.

"Who? I can't hear you, mate, you're breaking ... Billy? Hello?" The call ended before it had begun. It made little difference. Pete shrugged at Charlie, unable to say who or what the call was about.

The phone rang again. Pete jumped up to stand on a larger boulder nearby before answering the phone.

"Hello. Billy? Yep, I can hear you, mate. Can you hear me, all right?"

The call didn't last long. Ending the call, Pete turned to Charlie. "It was Billy. We need to go back."

"My brother, Billy?"

"Yeah, he said Cookie's looking for you."

Hope filled Charlie's eyes. It had to be Myra. He leaped to his feet. The tiredness leaving him, eager to return to their campsite. Pete followed close behind.

"Charlie, don't get your hopes up. Billy didn't say what Cookie wanted."

"They've found her. What else could it be?" he asked.

"Mate!" Pete grabbed his friend's arm and swung him forcefully to halt his enthusiasm.

"Simmo, it has to be."

"Not necessarily! Billy sounded pretty serious; not like he had good news."

Charlie's hope faded as he realised it could be anything: new evidence, more questions, who knew. He turned back to the track and began walking at a slower pace. There was no urgency to rush back to town and discover what was happening. This nightmare may never end.

A light covering of cloud had covered the sky. The birds darted swiftly as the threat of rain approached. By the time the pair reached their campsite and vehicle, a light drizzle fell. The day was still warm and muggy as they packed up the last of their equipment and began the journey back to town.

¥

The main street of town was all but empty. One car refuelled at the servo, two pedestrians stood talking in front of the supermarket, and Harold, the town drunk, lay sleeping under his thin blanket in the large concrete pipe the local kids used during the day as a bike jump in the park.

Occasional rays of sun shone through as the drizzle eased and clouds parted. Charlie Dixon trudged towards the police station with Pete Simmons.

As they entered, the familiar bell over the door announced their arrival. Police Sergeant Phil Cook appeared from the back office. Charlie noted the familiar posters, bench seat, and doorway he knew led to two cells at the back of the station and felt like a stranger. Filled with apprehension, he stepped up to the counter.

"I heard you were looking for me," he said.

"Hi Charlie ... Simmo. How about you come and have a seat?"

"How about you just spit it out? Have you found Myra?"

Phil Cook tilted his head and frowned at the man hoping for a miracle.

Phil had always liked Charlie. He was a good kid in his youth, never getting into any real trouble. He would be the first to put his hand up when something needed to be done, was a committed member of the CFA since his youth and typically the first to answer callouts. He hated being the one to give Charlie bad news. But he would hate it even more if someone else released it. Now, he had to do his job as a policeman as well as a friend.

"Charlie, the investigation's initial findings suggest the fire was not a complete accident."

"What do you mean?"

"The gas fittings weren't installed correctly."

"I put them in myself. With Billy–"

"I know." Phil cut him off, not letting him say any more. Even a professional didn't want a friend to incriminate himself.

"I thought the fire destroyed everything. What did you find?"

"Like I said, these are the initial findings. The investigations are continuing."

"So, you wanted to see me to tell me the investigation isn't finished, but some bastard thinks I had something to do with it?"

"Come on, Cookie," interjected Pete. "You know he didn't."

"Simmo, what I think is irrelevant. My job is to find out what happened."

"Is there anything else?" asked Pete, suddenly in 'lawyer mode' and sensing Charlie's eagerness to leave.

"Yeah. Two things. I have to ask Charlie not to leave town until the investigation is complete–"

"For fuck's sake..."

"And I need to ask you to identify a piece of jewellery."

Charlie looked at the police officer as his heart sank. He nodded tersely as the officer ushered him towards the back office. Charlie and Simmo sat at the desk Cookie pointed to before he left the room. It wasn't long before he returned with a small plastic bag. He withdrew a gold ring with a red ruby and matching necklace.

"Do you recognise these?" asked the sergeant, passing them to Charlie.

Charlie examined them, turning them over in his hands. He couldn't speak, recognising the jewellery he had given his wife on her birthday. *"Charlie, these are beautiful! But when am I ever going to wear them out here?"* She usually kept them safe in her jewellery cabinet, only taking them out and wearing them on special occasions.

"They were on one of the bodies, mate. I'm sorry."

Charlie couldn't remember Myra wearing the jewellery that day. But then, she'd wear them every now and again to make herself feel better. He had wondered if her emotional state after baby Issie's birth resulted from depression. She always said she was fine and would put on a brave face. But he knew the days he saw her wearing the ruby jewellery at home were bad days for her. It made sense that, after their argument, she'd chain the necklace and ring around her neck.

A hollow feeling engulfed Charlie. He felt detached from his wife for the first time.

Tears welled. Phil Cook forgot for a minute about being a police officer investigating a fatal house fire. With a hand on Charlie's shoulder, he comforted him as he mourned.

Charlie allowed the tears to flow for just a minute. Pulling himself together, he passed the jewellery back. All sorts of realisations flooded his mind.

"Charlie," Phil said hesitantly. "I think you need to get yourself a lawyer."

Pete stood beside his friend. His expression changed from a gentle sadness to hardened stoicism as the realisation sank in. Whatever was ahead for Charlie, he would be there with him.

Chapter Five

Outside, Charlie left the police station, walking as if in a trance, focusing on a destination and placing one foot in front of the other, trying to block out the noise in his mind. Questioning his involvement in the fire was unfathomable, but being suspected of murdering his family was incomprehensible. Simmo spoke, but Charlie had tuned out. He focused on proceeding in the direction he was led and quietening his mind.

Billy stood enjoying the warm summer sun as he waited by the car. The street was all but empty as Charlie and Pete left the police station. Charlie looked like a beaten man. His glazed eyes barely acknowledging his brother as he moved towards the waiting vehicle. Billy could hear Simmo talking in hushed tones as he walked a pace behind and Phil Cook frowned as he watched the men walk away.

Charlie, scarcely aware of others speaking to him, ignored the voices. Billy reached for his brother's arm to guide him into the car. Simmo, having caught up, placed one hand on Charlie and reached to open the car door.

"Just get in, mate," he said.

Suddenly, Charlie pulled away and freed himself from the hands that gripped him.

"Enough!" he yelled. "Enough."

He turned from them and walked in the opposite direction.

"Charlie," called Pete.

"Let him go," replied Billy. "Let him walk. He won't go too far. Once this sinks in, he'll want answers, just like the rest of us."

"I'm trusting you two to keep a close eye on him," said Phil, who'd sidled up beside them. "And one of you get him a lawyer."

"I know a good one in the city. I'll contact him, Cookie. Can ya keep me posted?"

"I'll do my best, mate. But..."

"Yeah, I know, you're a copper. Your hands may be tied."

"For fuck's sake, you two. You're talking about Charlie. You've already questioned my integrity as a plumber, Sarg! Do I need a lawyer, too?" Billy barked.

"Get a grip, Bill." Pete's voice was stern yet gentle as he touched Billy's shoulder.

Billy shrugged the hand off and moved several steps away as he watched Charlie someway down the street.

A cool breeze lifted dust from the desolate roadway.

Charlie walked on the footpath to the end of the main street. As the concrete path ended and a dirt track beside the bitumen road began, he proceeded without noticing, intent on his private thoughts. Oblivious to the vehicles that passed on the road, he walked in a daze, attempting to reconcile the fact that his wife and baby daughter were gone. He thought about the installation of the gas lines. Had there been a mistake? Did he play a role in the incident? He and Billy had worked on it together. Wanting nothing but the best for his family, he hadn't taken shortcuts. He thought he had been meticulous.

His thoughts turned to the few facts he knew. Cookie had said the car hit the house and the driver thrown. But Isabella was in the lounge room. Why would Myra be in the car? Where was Myra going without the baby?

She was wearing the ruby jewellery.

"Oh, Myra. It was a bad day and I didn't realise. I'm so sorry," Charlie said as he looked at the perfectly blue skies through water-filled eyes and a golf ball-sized lump in his throat.

Charlie tried to pull the pieces together. Maybe she'd got in the car and realised she'd forgotten the baby. And that's when she quickly dashed back, hitting the house at high speed, causing the accident.

Another possibility entered his head.

"Surely not," he said.

Had it not been an accident? Did Myra intentionally plough into the house?

He was riddled with guilt at the thought. Their conversation about the stupid holiday when he'd dug his heels in and not let her have her way. Insisting on helping the school after the storm rather than going home as she'd asked. Was it a cry for help that he hadn't heard? Why didn't he insist on her seeing the doctor when he knew she was struggling with the baby? Why hadn't he taken her himself?

"Oh Myra, Myra, Myra! What have I done?" Charlie fell to his knees, allowing the twigs to pierce his skin, feeling the pain and hoping it would outweigh the agony in his heart.

¥

The call of a kookaburra roused Charlie from his sorrow. Charlie had walked from town and collapsed by the trees that stood as sentinels at the front gate of his property. Rising from the ground, he looked at the clearing where his house had stood. Now, nothing but grey and blackened ash marked where his world of happiness had been. He straddled the police tape that still surrounded the perimeter. His heart had a hole ripped out where love and two beautiful people had once lived.

A car pulled up the long drive and stopped by the shut gate. Pete and Billy got out, walking silently toward Charlie as he sat cross-legged on the ground by the once warm, homely chimney stack. Words were insufficient as they, too, sat silently staring at the charcoal scar before them.

Charlie eventually broke the silence.

"Something's not right."

"What d'ya mean?" asked Pete.

"I don't know. They've got it wrong. I think..." he hesitated.

"What?"

"I don't know," he said.

Billy and Pete turned to Charlie, who said no more. Despite their efforts to explain and reason, waiting for the investigation's completion was their only option.

Over the coming weeks, Charlie ruminated one possibility after another, coming to no satisfactory conclusion. He didn't believe Myra's emotional state was such that she drove into the house. Or consider their relationship so fractured that she could not talk to him. And he couldn't believe that he had inadvertently caused the accident. He'd return to the possibility that Myra and Issie weren't the bodies found in the ashes, that it was all a mistake until he remembered the ruby jewellery. The only thing that seemed to make sense, the jewellery found, brought him back to the facts before him.

The possibility of a gas installation mistake troubled him, but Billy insisted it wasn't the problem. He'd double-checked everything. They hadn't taken shortcuts or turned a blind eye. Billy was sure the investigation would prove this if nothing else. But Charlie struggled to come up with any other valid explanation for the tragedy.

While the people of the area voiced their refusal to believe Charlie had anything to do with the unfortunate events, no one could explain what had happened and the uneasy questions hung in the air.

Everyone waited with bated breath for the investigation to be completed and the truth to be known.

¥

The coroner's inquest took six agonising months to complete. All the while, Charlie felt stuck in limbo. There was no closure. No funerals were allowed for Myra and baby Isabella; by all indications, it may still be a while before they released the remains. Doubts, discussions and theories abounded. The day for the findings to be released couldn't come quickly enough.

Charlie hadn't slept well and was up before dawn to prepare for the day. Yet again, his existence felt surreal. He'd almost become used to living between realities and had all but forgotten how to exist in only one.

He hadn't been to work since the incident, unable to function or concentrate on anything for more than a few minutes.

Having nowhere else to go, Charlie stayed with Billy. He couldn't bear seeing the scorched earth and the constant reminder, so he avoided the heartbreaking site, only returning when summoned by authorities. He was more than happy to let nature reclaim his once-treasured plot.

For Charlie, everything rested on today's findings.

After making a mug of coffee, Charlie sat in the dark on the front veranda to await the coming dawn. He watched as the steam rose from his cup and evaporated.

The sky was dark except for a slither of grey on the horizon, where the sun was only just beginning to make its presence felt. Apart from a light breeze rustling through the trees, all was silent.

Charlie sat in tracksuit pants, letting the cool morning air chill his naked chest. He saw the hair on his body wriggle in the breeze and watched the goosebumps rise on his arms. It seemed an age since Charlie had felt anything. At no point was he inclined to think about finding a shirt or something warm to put on. Feeling anything other than hollow reminded Charlie he was still alive. The sensations generated a mix of satisfaction and annoyance. If only he could be like the steam over the coffee cup and evaporate...

The front screen door squeaked as Billy came outside, hands clutched firmly around a coffee mug. He sat on the top step and faced his brother, one leg stretched out across the threshold and the other bent to rest on the lower step. With his back against the railing, he also looked out into the dark pre-dawn. The stillness now breaking to the first of the bush choir's chorus.

"Where are you?" he finally asked.

"Nowhere," Charlie replied.

"It's pretty early."

"Yep. Couldn't sleep."

The two brothers sat in silence to watch the first light of day finally pierce the darkness. The silhouette of the nearby gum trees and chicken coop appeared.

The sun rested on the horizon when Billy rose without a word and took Charlie's mug. He disappeared for only five minutes before returning with two more steaming cups of coffee. The dawn had arrived in all its glory. The sky was clear and blue, with the few distant clouds tinged red by the coming sun.

"Red sky at night, shepherds delight. Red sky in morning ..." quoted Charlie.

"You worrying about today?"

"Worrying? No. I'll just be glad when it's over," Charlie replied as he blew the steam and watched it danced and swirled from his cup.

"It'll be okay. That lawyer, Hill, he seems to know what he's doing."

"I hope so."

¥

The sun was well over the horizon and the brothers were in the kitchen when Pete Simmons arrived to accompany them to the lawyer's office in the city. From the rumours in town, half the Yarra Valley were waiting with bated breath to hear the findings. Pete had kept as close an eye as possible on the investigation as it'd progressed. He looked with a lawyer's eye rather than a friend's. A lot was riding on the outcome: Billy's reputation as a plumber, Charlie's innocence, and the one no one wanted to talk about, the possibility of a criminal charge being laid.

Chapter Six

Oscar Hill, Charlie's lawyer, waited for his client, enjoying the winter sun beaming through the large window to warm his back as he read a lengthy document. For months, the coroner's office and Mr. Hill—isolating the exact cause of the devastating fire—had questioned Charlie.

A late blast of winter howled up Kavanaugh Street as Billy, Charlie and Pete walked toward Oscar Hill's office. The stark, officious building echoed the footsteps and hushed voices. Charlie shivered. This was what he'd been waiting for, he reminded himself.

"You right, mate?" asked Pete.

"Yeah. Yeah, I'm good. Let's go."

They met Oscar Hill at the courthouse at 10.30 a.m. and patiently sat in the reception area, waiting as the time ticked. Charlie sat with sweating palms and right leg jigging. He looked around the modern space. A dozen or more people also sat waiting; for what, Charlie wondered.

As he looked around, the door opened, and Myra's father, Alan Bennett, walked in. He had told Charlie he would be there, but it had slipped Charlie's mind. Myra's mother, Jean Cartwright, had decided it would be too much to sit and hear the details of her daughter's horrible death. Myra and Isabella were gone. That's all she cared about. Charlie was surprised, though, that his brother-in-law, Geoff, wasn't with Alan.

"Charlie. How you holding up?" asked Alan, concerned.

"As well as can be expected, I think," he replied, with a forced smile. "I thought Geoff would be with you."

"No. Not sure what the story is there, but he said he wouldn't be coming. Think he's spending the day with his mother. Probably a good thing," Alan said with his normal businessman tone and countenance.

A door opened as Oscar Hill and several officials signified the commencement of the hearing. Everyone stood as the judge took his place on high.

Over the next thirty minutes, the details of the incident were recounted. Every painful, minute detail retold.

"I have several things I wish to say," the judge surmised. To begin with, I almost postponed this hearing because of the lack of several crucial pieces of evidence needed to finalise the case. However, I also know that a young man sits in limbo, awaiting the outcome of my findings. Therefore, I have allowed the case to be heard today.

"There's no doubt that the intense and explosive fire caused the death of two people. The adult in this tragedy showed injury to the skull, collaborating with the theory that this person was the driver of the vehicle and thrown from the car. Being so young, the infant would not have been in a position to do anything once the fire began and died from asphyxiation."

Billy and Pete could feel Charlie's agitation growing and simultaneously put a hand on Charlie, one on his leg, the other on his arm.

"A faulty gas conversion of the car caused the explosion, not a faulty gas fitting on the house, as speculated. It was pure bad luck that the vehicle hit the house gas mains rupturing the gas line."

While Billy and half the courtroom breathed an audible sigh of relief, Charlie remained ridged.

"I find no evidence to corroborate an unlawful act of wilful damage to property or the deaths involved. However—"

The judge hesitated as he prepared for the final statement. As he did, all in the courtroom held their breath. What more was there to say?

Sitting on the edge of his seat, Charlie slumped forward to stare at the ground. What? He thought.

"I am appalled at the examiner of the bodies that has failed in his duty of care. There is little doubt that the infant caught in this most tragic of events was that of Isabella Grace Dixon. But, the country examiner has made too many assumptions and not carried out his identification to my satisfaction. There were two fatalities in this event. Therefore, with a clear conscience, I cannot find that they were those of Myra Janine Bennett Dixon and Isabella Grace Dixon. I cannot comment on motive, or conceivable motive, until we clarify this crucial point."

The courtroom sat stunned. Not Myra and Issie? How could this be? If not them, then who? Who was in my house, thought Charlie? He was thrown further into hell instead of being relieved with the findings. Would this never end?

"I allowed the hearing today to impart the innocence of several men whose livelihoods would continue to be impacted if any more time was wasted. However, until the two bodies involved are identified sufficiently and as quickly as possible, I cannot sign off on this case. I will not have the drunken fool who oversaw this vital task continue in his position and will personally oversee the undertaking of a new autopsy. To the Dixon and Bennett families, I offer my sincerest apologies for the oversight of justice. We will reconvene in two weeks."

It had ended—at least for the time being.

The courtroom sat stunned as the judge and officials removed themselves from the court. Slowly, the audience began to move and make comments.

"I'm sorry, lad," said Oscar Hill. "It is good news that they have found no wrongdoing; that, at least, is something."

"No wrongdoing?" echoed Charlie. "If you ask me, a great wrongdoing has been committed."

The men stood as the courtroom emptied. Pete hooked his arm with Charlie's as he led him out to the corridors of the building and the waiting crowd. Many were lost for words as they approached Charlie, shaking his hand, offering condolences and congratulations to Billy.

As they headed up Kavanaugh Street to head home, Charlie turned and said, "She's not dead. I just know it."

Chapter Seven

Back in Gilderoy, Charlie knew he had to revisit the starting point if he was to find Myra. He insisted on going to the block, despite Pete and Billy arguing with him to leave it to the authorities.

As drizzle fell, Charlie walked around the scarred land. New growth was showing through the blackened trees and charcoaled scorched earth. Already, ground showed signs of the lush, fresh grass and ferns that would, with time, hide the painful truth. How cruel Mother Nature could appear, he thought. Her beauty would again replace the horror and tragedy he would live with–but that was life. Seasons changed and life moved on.

Charlie wept for Isabella; his precious little girl who would never grow old. He ached for the touch of her skin, the smell of her clean body, the sparkle in her eyes and the cheeky grin. As his thoughts turned to Myra, sure of her survival, numbness replaced the ache. If only she would reach out to him–wherever she may be.

None of it made sense. Who could the other body be if not Myra? No one could tell him. Who would have been visiting? Who would have been in their car? And why had they worn Myra's jewellery? His thoughts turned to Myra's family.

"Billy!" Charlie called.

Billy compliantly left the comfort and dryness of the car and came running along with Pete.

"Can you remember what Alan said about Geoff? Why wasn't he there today?"

"I can't remember, mate. Sorry."

"Wasn't he with Myra's mum?" added Pete.

"Seems absurd to me," said Charlie.

Pete and Billy waited patiently for Charlie, who appeared in deep thought, his brow furrowed as he stared at the ground.

"When the accident happened, he contacted me daily for weeks. Remember? He was just as shocked as the rest of us and wanted to get to the bottom of it. Then he stopped calling. In fact, I can't remember the last time I spoke to him."

"Mate, don't get conspiracy theories in your head. Many people stopped calling."

"But not everyone was family. He knows something."

Charlie headed toward the car without waiting for the others to reply. Pete and Billy looked quizzically at each other before following.

"Where are you going?" asked Billy.

"Charlie, slow down. Wait for us. We'll come with you," said Pete, knowing there was no stopping him.

"If she's alive, surely her family knows where she is. Why did she leave Issie? I can cope with her walking out on me, but not our daughter."

"You don't know that she did, Charlie! Listen to yourself," pleaded Billy.

"I'm going to see Geoff," he stated emphatically.

The three men jumped in the car, Pete insisting he drove, to Charlie's annoyance. The way Charlie was, there was no way Pete would let him behind the wheel of a car.

Thunder cracked through the darkening clouds as the weather turned nasty.

Speculation occupied the twenty-minute drive. Was Myra at Geoff's? Was she with her mother? Did they know where to find her? Maybe she had died in the blaze. What about a funeral? Had he thought about when? His friends relentlessly attempted to keep Charlie from moving too far away from the reality they knew. Two people were dead, most likely his wife and daughter. But Charlie wouldn't talk about funeral arrangements. He was on a mission. Sure she was alive, he would find Myra and get the answers he needed.

When they arrived at Geoff's home, he didn't seem surprised to find the three men standing on the doorstep in the pouring rain. He ushered them inside, offering them something warm to drink.

"Sorry I couldn't be there today," Geoff offered. "But Mum was in a bit of a state. Knowing Dad would be there, I thought it best to stay with Mum."

"Do you know where she is?" Charlie asked, cutting to the chase.

"Gees, Charlie, don't you think I'd have said if I knew anything?" he rebuffed.

"No." Charlie glared at the other man, knowing many times that he'd protected his twin sister with a lie.

"Okay, settle down, Charlie," said Pete, stepping in.

"Simmo, I don't appreciate your mate coming into my house and accusing me of something I know nothing about," said Geoff.

"Charlie's upset. He's had a shock. Don't take it personally," said Pete.

"A shock! I've had more than a fucking shock! I've had enough of this. I want answers," yelled Charlie, standing to tower over his brother-in-law, spilling his coffee as he did.

"Easy, mate!" said Geoff, not backing down from the anger. "Why are you doing this?"

"You two had that ... ESP, twin thing. Can you feel her? Can you look me in the eye and tell me you believe she's dead?" Charlie asked.

Silence fell on the room as Geoff hesitated before answering.

"No. I can't," he finally replied.

"You think she's alive?" asked Pete.

"I don't know what to think," said Geoff, turning to pace the floor. "Mate, I wish I could help you. I wish I could give you answers. But I can't." Geoff remained looking away from the others.

Silence again filled the room. The only noise was the loud hammering of the rain on the tin roof and the occasional roll of thunder.

The front door burst open, shattering the silent hold on the room as Alan entered.

"Boys," he said, surprised by what he confronted. "Everything all right?"

"Yeah, Dad. Charlie thought I may know something of Myra's whereabouts."

"Ah, Charlie. You've got to let this go. I know it's hard, but the autopsy will confirm she was in the fire. You need to get your head around it. It's been months! Don't you think if Myra were alive, she would have contacted one of us by now?"

"Alan's right, Charlie," added Billy.

"Look, I've been speaking with Jean. We know this has been tough for you and coming to terms with the loss, so we'd like to offer to take care of the funeral arrangements if you'd let us."

Charlie stared in disbelief.

"Think about it," continued Alan. "Let's wait out the two weeks until the identities have been formally confirmed, and then we can talk again. Come on, son. Sit down. Relax."

Charlie didn't reply as he headed for the front door.

Pete apologised for Charlie's behaviour and followed his friend out to the car.

¥

The two weeks finally passed and the men returned to the coroner's court for what they hoped to be the last time. There was no waiting for the coroner, who arrived and began proceedings on time.

"I am satisfied with the completion of the autopsies on the two bodies and can confirm," he began, "the identity of Isabella Dixon, aged seven months. I can also confirm the second body."

The room fell silent. Charlie felt faint as he realised, he was holding his breath. He felt an arm around his shoulder. He waited.

"The second victim was of Maree Elizabeth Saunders, 26 years of age, last known address 57 Daly Street, West Brunswick. Not Myra Janine Bennett Dixon, as previously suggested."

Murmurs of shock and surprise filled the courtroom. Charlie turned to Pete to clarify, "Not Myra?"

"Not Myra, mate."

"I knew ..." he said, turning away. "But my Issie G ..." Charlie sobbed for the loss of his daughter. For months, he'd held out a hope that neither body was Myra or Issie. To finally hear one was his daughter was both a relief and a tragedy. He was powerless to comfort her, alone in the darkness of death. His little princess. He had silently comforted himself that they were together if they were both dead. Now, his daughter was alone.

When finally he looked up, the court was almost empty. The coroner had gone with the proceedings finished. Beside him sat his brother, friend and official, who ushered him to a private room.

"What do I do now?" he asked absently.

"You bury your daughter and let the police keep looking for Myra. If she wants to be found, she will be."

Charlie left the building feeling somewhat numb but angry. He didn't know where Myra was or why she'd gone. He didn't know if she was all right or hurt. One thing he knew, he couldn't forgive her for walking away from their daughter. He would bury his sweet little 'Issie G' and pour a lifetime of love into the ground to comfort her in her endless sleep until the day came to join her.

Charlie decided he wouldn't attempt to find Myra. If she could be so callous as to leave and torment him without a word, she wasn't the woman he thought she'd been. She was all but dead to him, he told himself.

"You don't wanna hear this, mate, but as they say, time is a healer. We'll get through it together," promised Pete.

"Ditto," added Billy.

Chapter Eight

Charlie returned to The Valley a changed man. The sun would never beam as brilliantly again, always overshadowed by a grey cloud. His world had been torn apart, but he had to keep living. His first job was to bury his daughter—a task he'd never anticipated.

Hundreds turned out for Isabella's funeral. He sat in the chapel's front row as the service took place. Everyone who attended, including friends, family and acquaintances, shed tears together. But Charlie couldn't cry.

He stood to give the eulogy. "She should have recently celebrated her first birthday," he said. "She should have been walking around this chapel today, wondering what all the fuss was about. But she's not. And while I'm sad she's gone, I can't help but celebrate my seven glorious months with her. Her little face and the way it would light up when I came home from work will never leave me. Her presence blessed my life. That little girl taught me more about love in seven months than I'd learned in thirty-one years. I can't be sorry about that. So, Issie G, thank you for coming into my life, our lives, and touching us the way you did. You will be dearly missed and forever loved. See you soon, hopefully."

Charlie, Billy, Geoff and Alan moved toward the tiny coffin to escort baby Isabella on her final journey and resting place while sniffs and sobs could be heard.

The chapel emptied as mourners greeted Charlie before heading to the Powlie Pub for the wake. Charlie sat alone with a photo of his daughter and toys to be placed around her grave.

"I'm sorry, little one. I let you down when you needed me most." Charlie paused. "If you get lonely, find your great-granddad. He'll no doubt be fishing somewhere and would love to have you sitting beside him—as long as you don't talk too much. That will scare the fish away," said Charlie with a smile, remembering his fishing trips with his grandfather.

Charlie felt comforted knowing his daughter would be with his grandfather, a gruff old man who tried to be scary but loved any young child. Issie G was in good hands.

¥

It would take time to pick up the pieces; Charlie knew that. The coroner's findings and the funeral had begun the first steps to moving on. The yoke that had hung around his neck for months was loosened. However, until Myra was found, he knew he would not rest.

Charlie returned to work the following week, no one more surprised than Charlie. He woke one morning to hear the sounds of Billy preparing to go to the gym. As he staggered toward the kitchen, still groggy from sleep, Billy invited him—as he did most days—to join him. This time, Charlie accepted the invitation.

He spent most of the time at the gym watching his brother work out. It had been years since Charlie had done a serious workout and most of the last eight months doing very little at all. He couldn't do half the training he would have been capable of a year earlier. Billy continued to be encouraging, regardless of what Charlie achieved. Being there was a positive step forward, advised Billy.

At seven-thirty, Charlie and Billy exited the gym. With Billy going to work and Charlie planning to head back home, he suddenly changed his mind, deciding to have breakfast and head to the office.

As he arrived just after nine o'clock, Charlie was greeted with a teary hug from the older receptionist, Marg and handshakes and 'welcome back' from other colleagues. Charlie's manager, Gerard, pulled him aside and before long Charlie had a small workload and instructions to "only do what you feel up to."

Charlie sat in his office looking at the familiar things around him as if seeing them for the first time. He felt like an intruder in someone else's life. He remembered how Myra would call him through the day if she were bored, when she called to say Issie G had smiled for the first time, that she'd rolled over for the first time and when she sat by herself. Sometimes, she held the phone to Issie's ear and Charlie spoke to her while she gurgled or snorted and breathed loudly. It took all his willpower to switch off the memories and concentrate on doing his job.

Marg popped her head in regularly throughout the day to ask how he was; did he want anything, could he find everything he needed? And to advise where things had moved to in his absence. While her brief visits were a waste of time, Charlie was thankful for them. She'd always been the unofficial office-mother, clucking around after all her 'chicks', and today he appreciated it.

Charlie made it through the day. He doubted he'd been productive, but he'd stayed. As he packed up, his mobile phone rang.

"Chuckles, it's Simmo. Heard you were back at work. Well done. How'd you go?"

"Just packing up now, Simmo. Fancy a beer?" Charlie asked warmly.

"Would love to, mate. But having dinner with Mum and Dad; Mum's birthday."

"Ah, give her a kiss for me."

"She'll like that. I could call in after dinner if you like? Have a beer with you on my way home?"

"Yeah, okay. As long as you're not too late. Some of us have to work tomorrow," Charlie laughed.

"Cheeky bastard! I work!"

Charlie laughed for the first time in what felt like a long while. It felt good.

He was halfway to the car when the mobile rang again.

"Charlie, it's Cookie," said the police sergeant apprehensively.

"Cookie. Hi. What can I do for you?" Charlie asked calmly.

"I was hoping we could have a chat, you know, clear the air."

"It's okay, Cookie. I know you were doing your job. No air to clear. It's just going to take me a little while to get back to some sort of normal."

"Yeah, I know. One drink. Powellie Pub in five minutes. Wha'dya say?"

"Okay. One drink. Don't wanna get done for drink driving or anything."

It was the sort of comment the old Charlie would have made. He tried it on to see how it felt. It felt false, like he was reciting a line from a movie he'd once seen. But it made Cookie laugh. Maybe there'd be a lot of play-acting for a while as he re-adjusted.

Charlie sat at the pub waiting as a new thought entered his mind. He could ask Cookie on how best to find Myra.

Sergeant Phil Cook came to the table with two beers and a packet of potato chips. As he set the glasses down, Charlie stood to shake his old friend's hand. The look of regret on the other man's face was unmistakable and Charlie tried to make it a little easier for him. They spoke of the goings on in the region: events on local farms, the B&B still recovering from damage during the big summer storm, the local football team and how they'd done so well in the last season even without their star forward. They spoke about anything light and shallow, which rarely happened in the past. Charlie was more than happy to wind up the older policeman with sometimes inappropriate statements. It had been a game that they willingly played. Today, however, they stuck to safe subjects for as long as Charlie could. Eventually, the conversation turned to finding Myra.

"Cookie, I wanna ask you something?" Charlie began.

Instinctively, Phil Cook adjusted his seat as he waited for the question.

"Where do I start looking for her?" Charlie asked.

"You know what my answer's going to be, Charlie. Leave it to the police," Phil replied.

"And you know what I'm going to say to that," Charlie replied.

"Yeah, I got a pretty good idea."

"Well, then?"

"My advice, Charlie–off the record, of course–you could try a private investigator. Put an ad in newspapers. Put one online. There're organisations around that can help."

"Yeah, money's an issue at the moment. But I could try the online thing. And what about the police? You guys getting any closer to finding her?"

Phil Cook shook his head.

"Nothing. She just vanished. I'm not saying any of this, but it's like she doesn't want to be found."

"Have you been looking?"

"She's reported missing, Charlie. Has been for some time now. But, you know how it is, if she doesn't want to be found..."

"Just doesn't make any sense," said Charlie, feeling the anger rise as his fist hit the table. "Why wouldn't she want to be found?"

Cookie shrugged his shoulders and shook his head. Neither could fathom it.

The two men talked for a while longer before Charlie, tired after a long day, ended their session. He was glad that he'd attempted to reconnect with Phil. He was a good man and Charlie knew he would do his utmost to find Myra.

Charlie left, pausing momentarily on the road by the side of his block of land before continuing to his brother's house. He decided he would speak with Simmo and Billy about looking for Myra and ask them to help.

By the end of the evening, the men had left messages with several missing persons groups and registered Myra's details. Charlie had also created a list of places she loved and may have gone to. He'd start working his way through the list tomorrow.

Chapter Nine

Charlie searched every lead he had. He contacted old friends of Myra's, talked to her family, and took drives to her favourite haunts. He even took a plane to Brisbane for a weekend search of her old stomping ground from when she was a child. Myra had always talked about how happy they'd been living in Brisbane before her parent's divorce. But she wasn't there. She wasn't anywhere. Every road seemed to be a dead end.

Christmas was just around the corner. Months of searching for Myra had turned up nothing for Charlie or the police.

Charlie arrived at the block on a Saturday afternoon to cut the grass before summer and snakes took over. He had come from the cemetery after his regular visit to Issie's grave and was tinkering with the ride on mower when Phil Cook pulled up.

"Cookie. This is a nice surprise," said Charlie.

"How ya doin'?" he asked.

"Okay. Just went to see Issie G. A few more toys and trinkets around the plot. Not sure who's visiting her, but it's beginning to look like a toy store around her grave," Charlie smiled.

"Yeah, I know a few of the locals have been visiting her. And all the kids seem to think it's nice to take her a toy," replied Phil Cook.

"You look like you've got something on your mind. Everything okay?" Charlie asked.

"Charlie, there's no easy way to say this, so ... brace yourself."

Charlie stopped what he was doing to face the police sergeant.

"I'm assuming this has something to do with Myra? Okay, I'm listening."

"She doesn't want to be 'found'."

"What do you mean? Has she been found?"

"I don't know any details because I asked them not to tell me. I hope you understand why. But when a missing person is located, if they don't want their whereabouts reported to anyone, the police have an obligation to keep it private."

"She's my wife? You're telling me I'm not allowed to know where she is?"

"Yes. Sorry, Charlie."

"And you didn't ask?"

"It's a privacy matter, Charlie. If she doesn't want anyone to know where she is, she's an adult and can make that choice. The police's job is to find her. We found her. She's safe. That's all I can tell you."

"For fuck's sake!" said Charlie, turning with disbelief from the sergeant. "What about her parents? Her mother, does she know any more?"

Phil Cook shook his head. Myra wants contact with no one.

Charlie paced trying to understand why Myra would do this and if Phil was holding out information.

"If I knew, Charlie, as a friend I'd tell you. But that would comprise me as a copper. I don't know anything other than she's safe and doesn't want to return."

Exasperated, Charlie walked in circles, waving hir arms and cursing in disbelief. Phil listened, nodding in agreement when it felt appropriate. There was nothing more to say. Clarity and understanding were not possible.

Phil helped Charlie carry tools to the shed, ready for use. As they put the equipment down, Charlie turned toward the river. The tranquil sounds of the water running over the rocks in the shallow stream did nothing to relax him. He stood, hands on hips, huffing and puffing in the early afternoon sun.

"What are you going to do?" Cokkie asked.

Charlie didn't answer immediately.

"Not much I can do, really. I can keep trying to find her or walk away."

The two men stood in silence for a few moments.

"What would you do?" Charlie asked, turning to his friend for guidance.

"Well, I guess ... This might sound harsh, Charlie, so forgive me. If I'd been through what you've been through and my wife didn't want to see me, then it says something. She isn't thinking straight about your feelings or about your loss. She's been through a lot, too, and is suffering in her own way. Maybe she's being self-centred. Maybe she'll come around. Who knows. But don't let her hold you back. You're young, get on with living!"

Charlie paced the fading scorch-marked perimeter of the old house, now hard to see through the high grass that had grown over it in the spring.

"I know you, Charlie. You standing there, pacing, thinking, 'how do I get closure if she doesn't want to see me?' "

Charlie nodded.

"You just have to decide to put one step before the next and keep moving. There is nothing you can do about her decision. If you want to track her down, go for it. But I think it's a waste of energy. She doesn't want contact, Charlie. Time to move on."

Charlie snorted. "And what do I do with this place?" he said, pointing towards the property. "I kept it so she'd know where to find me if she wanted to. She doesn't want me, so what do I do with this?"

The policeman hesitated before saying what was on his mind. "This is your home! You rebuild for *you*," he said.

Charlie stopped pacing to look at his friend as if the thought had never entered his head. He turned to survey the block, now resembling the surrounding wild bush environment more than a home.

Charlie had to make difficult choices. And that would take time, he thought.

Chapter Ten

The new house Charlie planned was smaller than the last one and situated closer to the river. He'd always wanted to build close to the river with visions of a deck where he could sit in the evening and listen to the water flowing. Myra had insisted on extending the existing cottage to ensure their children's safety away from the river. Charlie didn't see children in his life anymore, so was happy to build in his preferred area.

He often wandered the block wondering what the point of any of it was. The words of others rang in his mind, 'One foot in front of the other.' Like it or not–ready or not. He got the lawn mower ready to fulfil the task he'd come to do–cut the grass and mark out where the house would go.

The block had been left to Mother Nature since the incident and the grass on the three-acre site was long. Jumping on the ride-on mower, he began. Up and back. Up and back. Mowing systematically while lost in thought. As the mower finally reached the scorched house site, he stopped. With the engine still running, he sat. He hadn't crossed onto the site where his daughter and a stranger had died. He struggled to run over it with the mower, feeling as if by doing so, he would be removing the last of his daughter. Charlie felt sick.

His thoughts turned to Myra, and mixed feelings of love, anguish and anger returned.

"Myra!" he bellowed.

His heart sank and feelings of loss overwhelmed. Thinking about Myra would do him no good. Instead, his thoughts returned to Isabella. She would have been running around by now. He could almost see her playing by the big gum tree as he cut the grass, sitting in a swing hanging from the tree, calling for him to push her. Or sitting on the ride-on mower with him 'helping' daddy cut the grass. She would call him Daddy and speak to him in gibberish. And he'd be happy.

But that wasn't the way their story panned out. She wasn't here and never would be, he reminded himself. He had to choose whether to stay on the block, see the ghost of his daughter and feel the pain of his loss regularly, or sell up. No other tangible alternatives were available. If he kept the block now, it would have nothing to do with giving Myra a point to find him. She had chosen to leave.

He knew he couldn't leave The Valley, even if he wanted to. This is where his roots were. His family, his daughter. He could no more leave her than fly to the moon. Then, he concluded, there was no decision to make. This had been Issie's home. He'd build her beautiful garden and play area as a shrine. A place for her spirit to roam. A place where he could come and be with her. This was sacred ground. He couldn't let someone else come in and build on it. Not in Issie's garden.

Charlie reversed the mower, smiling as he moved closer to the sacred ground. The old house site was to become a memorial garden for his daughter. He planned to put in a swing and play equipment surrounded by a beautiful garden full of colour for other children when they visited. "Issie, Daddy's gonna build you a garden with swings and a playhouse. You can come here anytime you like to say hello."

With that, Charlie moved the mower forward and crossed the boundary. As he mowed the block, he thought about Issie's garden and how he'd create it. Where her body had laid, he'd put in a bird feeder and bath with a plaque announcing Isabella's Bird Sanctuary. A bench seat where he could sit and talk to her would surround the plaque. In time, there would be a small playhouse and a swing hanging from a tree yet to be planted. Around the perimeter of the garden would be a white picket fence. Inside the white picket fence, a herb garden and native flowers that would bloom around Isabella's birthday. Something he had planned and looked forward to tending with his daughter before the tragedy.

He would not let Myra spoil his life any more than she had. Her name would always remind him of sadness and loss, but he would honour his daughter and cherish the time he had spent with her.

Chapter Eleven

Charlie worked hard at the block. He'd found something to focus on that gave him a small amount of comfort. Through summer, he spent many of his spare hours preparing the ground for the building works that would begin in the new year and creating his daughter's garden. Once a week, he went to the cemetery and spoke to Isabella about the progress. For him, she couldn't be more real. While others worried he was hanging on to the past, he ignored their comments.

Summer passed and the cooling days of autumn saw the new house taking shape. As with the original house, he only used builders and craftsmen he knew. He also insisted on being a part of all the work as it happened. He didn't care if he acted as lackey cleaning up or as labourer, painstakingly bringing wheelbarrow after wheelbarrow of bricks and tiles the 100 metres from shed to site. Charlie worked like a man possessed.

Charlie was sitting cleaning second-hand bricks ready for use in the coming days when Pete arrived. So intent on his task, he failed to hear the car or see the man walking towards him.

"Gees, surely you can pay a teenager a few bob to do that job, mate?"

Charlie looked up and smiled. "Why, when I can do it myself?" he responded.

In a serious tone, Pete asked, "Money that tight?"

Charlie laughed, "No! Not quite. I'm doing it because I want to. I want to sit on my deck in years to come and boast about how I built this place."

"Fair enough, then," said Pete, offering Charlie a beer. "It's getting a bit dark, don't you think? Might be time to knock off."

"Yeah, probably. What are you doing out this way? Come to be the dutiful son and pay the folks a visit?"

"Come to be the dutiful friend and check on you!" he replied. "Haven't heard from you for a while and I was getting worried."

"Ah, I'm good, mate. No need to worry."

"Billy said you'd been spending a lot of time out here. You've evidently made peace with things."

"Don't know if I'd go that far, but being here, I feel closer to Issie. She's still here. Not sure if I'm looking after her or she's looking after me," he laughed.

"Well, looking at what you've built over there, who can blame her? Any kid would kill to spend time in there," he said before pulling himself up. "Sorry, mate. That was probably a bit insensitive."

"It's okay. You're right. When Jacko comes to work on the house, he brings his kids. They like the maze path. And when they're not playing in there, they like to try catching yabbies in the creek or kicking the footy. Plenty of space for them."

"Speaking of footy, Billy told me the season starts up soon. You thinkin' of playing this year?"

"Ah, don't think so. Too busy here."

Pete said nothing as he studied his friend.

"Simmo! Don't give me that look."

"What? I didn't say anything."

"You didn't have to," Charlie said, taking a large swig of his beer. "I know what people are saying and thinking. He spends all his time there talking to his dead daughter. I'm not hearing voices. I know she's gone, mate. And I'm okay with it–kinda. It comforts me to watch the house go up and the garden develop. Feel like I'm moving forward. You know?"

“Yeah, I get it. Just wouldn’t hurt you to socialise a bit more. A man can’t live in the wilderness on his own all the time. Especially a young man. You should be out–”

"Stop! I'm fine. I 'socialise' all day at work. If I need more than that, I know where to find everyone."

"Why don't you come to the pub with me tonight?"

"Powellie Pub? Nah, don't think so. Not up for a night of everyone asking how I'm going."

"Then come and stay at my place the night. We can go into one of my locals."

"Not tonight, mate."

"Charlie, I will not take no for an answer. I've already spoken to Billy and Macca and the others. They're up for it. Come on. We'll go back to Billy's. You can dust yourself off, and we'll head to mine."

"Rachel gonna be there?"

"Nah, we're not together anymore."

"Gees, that didn't last long! She must have been a bright one to work you out so quickly," Charlie laughed.

"Ease up, Chuckles! It was me that pulled up stumps! A little too alternative for me."

Charlie laughed as the men joked about Rachel's regular reading of Tarot cards that never seemed correct and crystals all around the house. Both decided Pete was better off without her.

Finishing their beers, Charlie agreed to have a night with his mates and they prepared to leave. It might lift Pete's spirits after the split from his latest lady, and it might get people off his back for a while.

As they passed Isabella's garden, Charlie whispered, "Night, Princess. I'll be back tomorrow."

Pete ignored it, allowing his friend to deal with his grief in his own way.

Pete left Charlie with Billy as they agreed to meet at his house in an hour. Billy asked the obligatory questions about Charlie's day and how far he'd gotten on the block, promising to come and give him a hand.

Charlie was soon cleaned up and ready to socialise. Anxiety and butterflies filled him. He looked forward to the night out–for the first time in a long time–but a level of guilt gripped him. He was enjoying life while his daughter didn't. He had banished the thoughts as he realised he had been spending a little too much time on his own and looked forward to a night of banter.

They'd no doubt play pool or darts, drink too much and all wake up with sore heads the next day. He gradually relaxed as he thought about it, allowing himself to take the next day off if needed. He'd cleaned enough bricks to keep the bricklayer going for at least a week. It wouldn't hurt him to have a break.

At Pete's local pub, the boys let their hair down. Six men were soon pleasantly intoxicated and the noise level rose. Charlie drank more than usual and was soon slurring his words, much to everyone's amusement. The Australian Snooker Championship, as they called it, was underway. The tournament followed a round-robin format, where the player who lost was eliminated.

They played old-school Australian music on the jukebox and sang at the top of their voices when Cold Chisel's *Khe Sanh* came on. All grabbing a pool cue to sing into as a mic. At one point, Simmo and Billy climbed onto the small table to dance before a bouncer stopped them. As they climbed back off the table, Simmo lost his balance, falling into the bystanders and knocking them to the ground.

"Okay, fellas," said the bouncer. "I think you've had enough. How about I call you a taxi to take you home?"

"Home? I don't have a home," said Charlie.

"Yes, you do, wanker. You're staying with me tonight," chimed Pete.

"Nah, mate. I think I'll go to the block, like our friend here says. I can sleep ... I can sleep in the garden," he said. "I can piss on the lemon tree nice and early in the morning to help it grow!" he said enthusiastically. "How good would that be?"

"Mate, you're talking shit!"

"Nah," Charlie continued, "Piss is good for lemon trees."

"We know! Every time you're drunk, you tell us!"

“Well then you should do it,” said Charlie.

“Don’t worry, mate. There’ll be plenty of time to piss on your lemon tree –hang on. You haven’t even planted the bloody thing yet! How about you wait till you plant it and then you can piss on it? Until then, you’re comin’ home with me,” said Pete.

The men exploded with laughter, including Charlie.

“Gees, sorry, Simmo. I got a bit confused.”

“It’s okay, mate. Don’t you look at me like that! You’re gonna tell me you love me, aren’t you?”

“I do love you, Simmo. You’re a good man. I don’t care what anyone says, you go all right.”

“Fuck me! I haven’t seen you this drunk in years. Come on boys, if I know this man, next he’ll be cryin’ about the cat they had as kids that disappeared.”

“It didn’t disappear,” said Billy. “Dad accidentally drove over it.”

“What the fuck, Billy!” cried Charlie. “All these years, you knew that and didn’t tell me!”

“Strewth, here we go. I have told you!”

“I loved that cat,” Charlie wailed. “I’ll never see her again.”

"It was a 'he', Charlie."

"No, my girl," he said, suddenly sombre. "I'll never see her again."

The men went quiet as they realised Charlie's drunkun thoughts went elsewhere. The men left the bar, Billy on one side of Charlie and Pete on the other.

"I'll never forgive her, you know."

"Hey, come on. We've had a great night. Let's not get morbid now."

The friends stumbled up the street without speaking for some time before, unexpectedly, Charlie began to hum and mumble.

"*I left my heart to the sappers round Khe Sanh. And I sold my soul with my cigarettes to the black market man.*"

"Ah ... mmm... I forget the words," he said, beginning to dance. "*I've travelled round the world... mejsa ie. What's the fucking words? Doesn't matter. The last train outta Sydney's almost gone ...*"

"Train? Mate, it's plane."

"Nah, train–isn't it?"

Charlie had forgotten his sudden moment of sadness as he and his friends argued their way up the street. The words of the well-known song varied from one addled mind to the next.

"Ah, who cares?" said Charlie, resigned to the fact that he had no idea what the words were. "I don't know. Can we look them up when we get to your joint, Simmo?"

"No!" Simmo said. "When we get home, I'm goin' to bed. And so are you!"

¥

Pete's lounge room looked like a war zone the following day. Bodies lay where they fell on sofas, armchairs and the floor. Charlie woke with the strong smell of Pete's dog in his nostrils. As he moved his aching head, he realised Toby's dog bed had become his pillow overnight. Sensing Charlie stirring, Toby slept close by and looked at him without affection, being forced to sleep on the cold floor rather than in his padded mat.

Charlie looked around to see Macca and Drongo cuddled together, still sleeping on the sofa bed. He smiled, making a note to rib them about it later. Slowly, Charlie raised his stiff body from the floor to sit in an armchair. On the next recliner, Vinnie lay awkwardly. Legs dangled off the footrest, head lolling on an angle and arms crossed. That's gonna hurt, thought Charlie. Hearing mumbled voices in the next room, Charlie went to be investigating.

Billy and Pete spoke softly at the kitchen table, sipping on coffee. Both looked a little the worse for wear.

"Morning, Barnsey," said Pete, smiling.

"Barnsey?" queried Charlie.

"Yeah. I think you sang more Cold Chisel songs last night than Jimmy Barnes has ever sung!"

"Oh, Gees. Yeah. Sorry about that."

"Don't be sorry, you were hilarious!" quipped Billy.

Pete got up to get his friend a drink and invited him to join them at the table. The other three men surfaced as they sat retelling tales of the night before, disagreeing about who did what and who won the snooker competition.

Charlie announced his departure close to midday. When queried about where he was rushing off to, he became vague spouting a desire to shower and put on some fresh clothes. This time, he couldn't easily be talked out of sticking around for a barbeque and 'hair of the dog'. As he walked toward the front door, Pete followed.

"I know, mate. I remember."

Charlie stopped. He turned without a word to face his friend.

"It's the anniversary today. And it would be better if you spent the day with your mates rather than alone."

Charlie didn't know what to say. For a moment, he stood dumbfounded.

"How about we go with ya to the cemetery? We'll all go say hi to Issie G. Then we'll come back here for a barbie and a few beers."

Charlie thought about it for a minute before replying. "Can we have the barbie at the block? Feel closer to Issie there."

"Sure we can. If that's what you want."

¥

It didn't seem right that the sun shone so radiantly on such a dark day. The sun warmed his back as he stood at his infant daughter's grave. The bird's song sounded sweeter than ever, filling the muted earth with peace. A gentle breeze caressed their faces as they stood in silence.

Charlie had been standing solemnly for some time when he smiled. His friends turned towards him.

"She said it's time to go. Doesn't want me hanging around with dead people."

The others said nothing but looked at each other.

"Come on, she's gone to play in the garden. Let's go cook us up some 'roo."

Billy walked next to his brother, looking suspiciously out the corner of his eye.

"What?" asked Charlie.

"Just wondering..."

"No. I didn't hear Issie. I was imagining." He smiled when he saw Billy sigh with relief.

Having reached their cars, they left for the block. Charlie seemed to have turned a corner.

Chapter Twelve

The days became shorter as winter approached and work on the house came closer to completion. Since the anniversary of the accident, Charlie was spending less time at the cemetery and was gradually regaining a balance in his life. Working long hours at the office, spending more time with friends, hiking through his beloved forests and working on the house. Like any building project, there were obstacles and delays, but nothing that significantly bothered him.

He had returned to the football club, giving in to two or three people who badgered him into submission, helping and advising on how best to look after the ground with more sustainable methods. As the ground flooded in winter and became heavy underfoot, Charlie devised ways to drain the water, collect and store it for reuse in the dryer summer. He hated to admit it, but Myra had rubbed off on him.

Charlie met Col Brown through the football club. Col was the recently appointed manager at a nearby vineyard and winery at Stoney Creek. Col had spent the last five years in the Riverina district. He had studied Viticulture in central Victoria before landing his first job in a vineyard on one of the much bigger properties on the Murray River. When the opportunity arose to manage the property in the Yarra Valley, he jumped at the chance. Now that he was here, though, he realised just how different the two environments were.

The vineyard had twenty acres of vines growing various grapes and production sheds. Although not a large venture in The Valley, Col Brown had ambitious plans for it. Stoney Creek had been owned and run by an Italian family comprising three brothers. However, they were all getting older and recognised the need to get some younger blood into the place to bring growing and production techniques into the modern era. It had served the three Fiorini brothers well over the previous forty years, but everything looked tired.

Col had noticed the change in the football ground throughout the season. And while many local grounds deteriorated over winter, with the harsh treatment it received with thirty-six men wearing spiked boots running on it for six months, the Gilderoy football ground seemed to improve. He inquired why this was, and soon found out about the club's secret weapon: Charlie Dixon.

Col sought Charlie out and the two rapidly became friends. The pair were only too happy to discuss, for hours on end, the pros and cons of varying practices at the vineyard or any other property type, for that matter. Both men were firm conservationists and a disagreement was rare.

Charlie's new house was completed two weeks after the end of the football season. With no weekend sports getting in the way until the cricket season started in earnestness, anyone and everyone seemed to be at the block, helping to finish the last of the painting and paving or whatever was needed.

While friends attended to the odd jobs, Col and Charlie disappeared to Charlie's work shed-cum-weekend home where they regularly set up experiments to test hypotheses.

"You should go into business, Charlie."

"Don't think so, mate. Don't think I'd have time for anything more than I'm doing."

"Once the house is finished, you will have spare time on your hands. You should set yourself up as a consultant. I'd hire you. I've told the 'old boys' about you and they've asked several times if you'd consider coming to work for them."

"Thanks, but I don't think so."

"Well, just think about it."

The thought was tucked away with no further immediate thought necessary. Instead, the two men returned to the house just in time for the first celebratory beers to be opened. Except for a few minor touch-ups that Charlie could take care of himself whenever he wanted, the house was finished.

Soon, the workers' families arrived for a large community barbecue to celebrate a housewarming. Charlie delighted in seeing the younger children enjoying Issie's garden and cubby house. As a twinge of regret seeped in, three people picked Charlie up and carried him away.

"Simmo, put me down. What are you doing?" he asked as those around laughed and cheered at the procession.

"Billy," he pleaded, to no avail.

He immediately realised what was coming. The men carried him, one on each arm and one carrying his legs, away from Issie's garden, down past the newly finished house, toward the river.

"Don't you dare!" he called, beginning to squirm.

"This is a housewarming, mate. You know what that means."

"Yeah, we warm the house! Party's in the other direction!"

"Means the landlord has to take a dip!"

"Come on, Col. You wouldn't really–"

Before he could finish his sentence, the three men flung Charlie from the small pontoon anchored to the shore by a couple of thick ropes and floated on the water's edge. Charlie re-surfaced, coughing and spluttering as the cold water took his breath away. Dripping wet, he gasped.

"You buggers," he managed to say, flicking water at the crowd now assembled on the bank.

Everyone cheered and clapped as Charlie struggled through the muddy and rocky water back to shore.

“Chuckles, gimme your hand,” Pete said, laughing, stretching out his arm to pull his friend out of the water. Charlie reached for the helping hand, but instead of using it to help himself out of the water, he pulled with all his might. Pete went flying into the water. Billy and Col could see what was coming their way and sprinted away.

“Bastards,” called Pete as he swam back toward the pontoon.

“Only fair, Simmo,” said Charlie as he splashed water into his friend’s face.

The two pulled themselves back onto dry land where they sat, regaining their breath for a minute as the other party-goers moved on towards the barbeque.

“Reckon we need a bonfire now, mate, to dry off,” suggested Charlie.

They soon had the younger boys heading into the nearby bush to gather fallen branches and kindling to get a fire going. As they did, Charlie and Pete went into the house to change into dry clothes. Charlie lent Pete an old, pale blue tracksuit, rainbow shirt and colourful jumper. Pete looked at the outfit with raised eyebrows.

"Sorry, mate. It's all I've got," said Charlie, grinning.

"Really?" asked Pete. "Trip down memory lane to Ken Done designs and the 80s?"

Charlie laughed, "Or sweet revenge."

It was a good day, Charlie thought. As difficult as the last eighteen months had been, he counted himself lucky to have these friends and people in his life.

Chapter Thirteen

After moving out of the shed and into the house, Charlie felt a sense of loss. With no house to build, as Col had said, he had time on his hands. He'd often sit on the back deck overlooking the river, as he'd imagined doing while the house was being built but found it missing something. Without someone to share the beautiful tranquillity of the sun setting over the hills and the sounds of the water brushing over the rocks, he'd begun talking to the local kookaburras. He encouraged them towards the deck with raw sausage he'd leave on the railing. Then he'd wait. Over time, the birds learnt to trust him. He'd alternate between sausage meat for the kookaburras and seeds for the rosellas and galahs. They never disappointed, becoming friendly and trusting enough to eat from his hands.

Pete had been given a promotion and moved closer in to the inner city suburbs. He'd also met Lucy, a lawyer who seemed the Asian version of Pete. They'd met while working on a case one day. Both represented a non-English speaking Asian, Lucy as a translator and Pete as assistant barrister. They hit it off instantly, with their romance evolving unexpectedly fast. When Pete got promoted and had to move, he moved in with Lucy. That's when Pete's dog, Toby, came to live with him.

Charlie had been more than happy to take the dog. Two-year-old Toby, little more than a pup, loved the wide-open spaces of the block. And, with a bit of training, would grow to accept the galahs and kookaburras as visitors to be left alone and not playthings to be chased. Every so often, when Charlie wasn't looking, Toby would bark or chase the birds, but soon learned he must look remorseful when Charlie scolded him for it.

The relationship between Charlie and Toby flourished and it soon became hard for Charlie to believe Toby had ever been someone else's companion.

When Charlie went to work, Toby had the run of a good acre of land around the house. He could access the river, which he rarely did, as he seemed a little afraid of the water. He always took pleasure in barking at the wild ducks that swam past regularly and Charlie wondered what Toby would do if one of the ducks ever came within his reach. Charlie suspected he'd get the fright of his life and run to hide.

¥

The third anniversary of the accident had passed with a little less pain. Issie's garden had mature plants and hidey-holes for visiting kids. Charlie had settled into his home. And life went on.

As with the previous two years, Charlie and his friends gathered for a few drinks and the now annual snooker championship. But, as with everything in Charlie's life, this too was a little different this year. Instead of being at Pete's local pub, it would be held at the block in the shed where Charlie had set up a 'man cave' with a pinball machine, space invaders video game, pool table and bar. Instead of being just 'the boys', the wives and girlfriends insisted on joining in.

Much to everyone's surprise, Col brought the woman he'd been seeing secretly, Lenore, and his sister, Ruby. He'd deliberately kept both away from his single friends, he explained, with a grin. And with good reason. Lenore was a stunner. While his sister's name was Ruby, everyone soon began calling her Rusty. Col insisted Ruby had many skills, but all seemed a little rusty. She'd only been in The Valley a month or so and, while staying with her brother, still hadn't met many locals.

The night was balmy and warm enough for festivities, which included a spit roast, cooked over the firepit with makeshift cover. Everyone arrived in the early afternoon for a game of backyard cricket. Despite the space of Charlie's block, there was only a cramped spot for a game of cricket. The usual rules applied: if the ball went into the river or Issie's garden, it was six and out; four runs for hitting the clothesline, and being out if the ball landed on the roof of the house as it was compared to being caught by a fielder. With enough people to have eight-a-side, Phil Cook seemed the clear choice for umpire.

Thus, the two teams lined up. Col and Lenore, Simmo and Lucy, Jacko and Jacqui, Macca and Rusty on one team. Drongo and Kate, Reedy and Maggie, Billy and Nicky, Titch—so-called because of her lack of height—and Charlie on the other. Col's team were first to field and took their tactically positioned places around the ground—the women of both teams gravitating to the outfield as far as possible from actually having to catch the ball. Macca let the first bowl go as Drongo stood ready with the bat. However, as the ball made its way down the pitch, Toby intercepted and took it to Charlie. Everyone roared in protest.

"Charlie! This can't be happening," announced Macca.

"I near took the dog's head off as I charged the pitch," said Drongo.

"All right, all right. Sorry, boys. Toby! Here!" bellowed Charlie.

Toby was soon put on the back deck with no choice but to sit and watch the action from a safe distance, much to his displeasure. He paced the deck, barking and whining in protest.

It didn't take long for Charlie's team to be all out for 25 runs and teams swapped places. Titch, the tomboy of the girls, took the ball, insisting she could bowl as well as any man. She took a short run up and let a slow ball go. Simmo, in his arrogance, swung the bat, hitting the ball and sending it skywards, laughing as he did.

"You'll have to do ..." his words stopped as the ball landed on the roof of the house.

"Out!" yelled Cookie, holding up one finger to verify his decision.

Pete rolled his eyes, shook his head and left the ground to find a shady spot to finish his beer. Next, Rusty took the field, looking most uncomfortable. As the ball came toward her, she shied away.

"You can't do that! Cookie, that's illegal," yelled one of the women in protest.

"If she wants to leave her wicket unprotected, that's her choice," replied Cookie.

Col, replacing the out Simmo, bolted to his sister's side from the pitch. "You gotta guard your wicket. What are you doing? We've played this a million times in the backyard. You know how to play."

"The ball's coming a hell of a lot faster than you ever bowled it at me!" she said.

"Okay, don't think about it. Just ... just stand there, close your eyes if you have to, and swing. Six balls and it'll be the end of the over. Then it'll be my turn to face the ball."

"If I live that long!" she said, agitation in her voice.

"Take it easy, Titch. No Italian tempers or competitiveness today, thanks," called Charlie.

Titch made a face at him as she walked to take her next run-up. The ball was slower. Ruby closed her eyes and swung. As the bat hit the ball, it rose into the air, sailing past the clothesline, hitting the top of the picket fence before bouncing back and landing outside Issie's garden. Charlie chased it, but before he could reach it, Toby bounded past to retrieve the ball and obediently returned it to Charlie, who threw it back to Titch. Ruby and Col were safe, adding six runs to open their run tally.

The protests were coming thick and fast, though. Charlie's team had an extra 'player' on the field, with Toby acting as a fielder. Ruby insisted they could have effortlessly run eight had the dog not fetched the ball. Cookie had his hands full as eight people stood around him, yelling at him to adjudicate against the dog.

While the protests continued, Charlie rubbing Toby's head with affection and whispered in his ear with pride. Charlie didn't know how he'd got out of the deck pen but decided to worry about fixing it later. As he patted Toby, he seemed a little more out of breath. His eyes appeared glazed and his nose unusually dry. Charlie took Toby back to the deck and encouraged him to have a drink.

Cookie eventually had no choice but to side with the protestors and ask Charlie to make sure Toby stayed out of the way. As Charlie put Toby's bedding on the deck and again shut the gate, it didn't seem to be a problem. Toby settled himself on his bed, thoroughly uninterested in the game.

The game of cricket continued for a good hour before Umpire Cook called 'bad light' and took up the stumps. By that stage, the teams were down to uneven numbers, with all the women, except Titch and several men having long abandoned it.

Night had descended and the spit roast was ready. Everyone sat around the shed enjoying the meal, with banter flying about the game. When everyone had eaten their fill, the annual snooker championship began. The round robin was drawn up for any who wanted to play. Titch and Rusty joined forces to represent the girls. At the same time, the eight men called upon their usual partnerships: Simmo and Jacko, Charlie and Col, Macca and Drongo, Reedy and Billy, and once again, Cookie became the referee and scorekeeper.

The final between Titch and Ruby, and Simmo and Jacko, was imminent. As they set the table for the showdown, Charlie realised he hadn't seen Toby for some time. He went to find him. The gate on the pen had had been left open for Toby to join the party, but Charlie couldn't remember seeing him. He put it down to Toby sulking about being locked away. Reaching the deck, Charlie was surprised to find Toby still laying on his bed. Toby didn't move.

"What's the matter, boy?" he asked, approaching his dog.

Toby lay motionless and barely turned his glazed eyes to look at the speaker.

In the distance, cheers indicated the championship had ended. But Charlie's attention remained intent on his dog; surprised that Toby didn't get up to greet him as he normally would. Something was wrong. He hastened to turn on the outside light to get a better look at his dog and grew even more concerned. Charlie tried to get Toby to stand without success. He placed his hand under the dog's head, but it flopped around uncontrollably. Charlie felt sick.

"Come on, boy. What's wrong?" he pleaded.

Footsteps approached as Charlie tried to rouse the dog. Ruby crouched beside him and asked if everything was okay.

"I don't know. I came to find him and he was just ... lying here."

Ruby's vet training took over as she pushed Charlie aside to examine the dog.

"Can we get him inside? Under better light?"

"Sure," replied Charlie, instantly bending to pick the dog and his cushioned bedding up, taking him inside the house and placing him on the dining table. Charlie turned on every light possible and grabbed a standard lamp from his office to give Ruby a stronger, more direct light to examine.

As she looked over the dog, feeling his joints and muscles, she noticed the bite marks and a small amount of blood.

"He's been bitten," she said.

"By what?" Charlie asked.

"I'm guessing a snake. Look, two puncture wounds. You seen any snakes around the property lately?"

"I reckon I've seen two in about ten years!" he replied, attempting to recall recent times. "What do I do? I need to get him to the vet." Charlie panicked.

Ruby looked with surprise at Charlie.

"Charlie, you do know what I do, right? Calm down."

"Yeah–," he said with some embarrassment. "Oh shit. Sorry. I forgot. You're a vet. Guess I'm a bit worried about me boy. Don't suppose you have some anti-venom on you by chance?"

"Actually, I do," she replied. "It's for tiger snakes, but it'd be worth a try since we don't know what bit him."

"I reckon it's probably a copperhead. They're fairly common by the river. Come for the frogs. But I haven't seen any recently."

"Well, there is no anti-venom for copperheads, so we'll go with the tiger snake antivenom."

"How long does it take to kick in?" asked Charlie.

Ruby looked at the wall clock. "I'll stay the night, if you'd like, and keep an eye on him. We won't know for ... five six hours maybe," she replied.

"He's gotta make it," said Charlie. "I can't lose him, too."

Silence fell between them as they prepared for a long night. Outside, the party continued, oblivious to what was happening in the house. It was a good hour before anyone missed the pair.

The party revellers wearied. Phil Cook, who had not had a drink all night, said his goodbyes, wished Charlie and Ruby well with Toby and promised to call in the next day. The other guests, sobered after hearing about Toby, began the clean up before leaving or retiring for the night.

Ruby and Charlie remained awake, sitting closely by Toby's side as the others slept. Ruby had offered to stay with Toby while Charlie slept, but Charlie wouldn't have it. He wasn't going anywhere.

At three o'clock, Ruby checked Toby. There was no evident improvement. His breathing was still erratic, as was his heart rate, with eyes glazed and tongue lolling from the side of his mouth.

"The meds should have kicked in by now, shouldn't they? It's been four hours," Charlie asked. "Shouldn't he be responding?"

Ruby hesitated before replying, "Sometimes it can take a while. Depends on a lot of things: size of the snake, Toby's general health before the bite. He's not a big dog, so any bite would knock him about a bit. The good news is he hasn't gotten worse."

Charlie hadn't considered that and took comfort in these small things. Needing something to do to feel useful, Charlie offered to make coffee. Ruby accepted gratefully.

In the kitchen, Charlie filled the kettle and prepared the cups. He stopped suddenly as he realised he was making Ruby's coffee the way he would have for Myra. It was a strange realisation. While Myra was never far from his mind, he wasn't sure what had prompted this thought. He put it down to tiredness. Turning to ask Ruby the question about her how she had her coffee, he found her standing in the door watching on.

"Ah, saved me a walk," he said, agitated. "How do you have your coffee?"

"Black, one sugar," she replied, looking at him intently.

"Right." Charlie, looking nervous, went back to start her coffee over again.

"You really love that dog, don't you?"

"He's my world."

"Col said it was Simmo's dog until a few months ago? Is that right?"

Charlie nodded.

"They say a dog is man's best friend. It might actually be the other way around in this case," she said, moving further into the kitchen. "It's lucky you found him when you did."

The big wooden dining table sat in the middle of the rustic yet modern room. Ruby looked around, taking in the bamboo bench tops, luminous gloss cupboard fronts, and white tile splashback. She sat at the table as Charlie finished making the coffee. He passed her the mug and sat on the other side of the table.

"Charlie, Col told me a little of what happened to your family."

"I'd prefer not to talk about it if you don't mind," he said guardedly.

"No, no. I don't want to talk about it either. Sorry, I didn't mean to make it sound like I was prying. It's just ... I can see if anything happens to Toby, it's going to rock you. But I don't want to make any false promises. If Toby was bitten by a copperhead, tiger snake, or even an eastern brown, he has a fight on his hands. I will do all that I can for him! I promise you that. But, there's no guarantee."

Charlie took a deep breath and looked at the stranger sitting opposite him. He'd put the life of his best mate into the hands of a stranger. What did he know about her? Col had told him about his little sister. He knew she'd finished her vet degree only five years earlier and had been working with the zoo. She was ambitious but didn't have a lengthy CV with experience having opened a vet practise since arriving in The Valley. He also called her Rusty because her skills weren't always up to scratch. Suddenly, he wondered if he should have taken Toby to his local vet, a man he'd known for years and knew to be good at what he did.

"I know what you're thinking." Ruby cut into his thoughts. "I should have taken him to the local guy. I know what I'm doing, Charlie. And I'm pretty sure the local vet wouldn't have made a house call or offered to stay up with you all night," she said with a smile.

"You're right. I'm sorry—again! I've known you a whole twelve hours and already seem to make apologies on a regular basis. I trust you," he said, unconvincingly.

Ruby laughed. "No, you don't! But that's okay. If you'd rather contact your local guy, just say the word. I won't be offended."

"No, Dr. Burn would have done the same as you, I know that. Now it's up to Toby to fight."

Ruby sat opposite him and smiled. She sipped her coffee, burning her tongue, and grimaced in pain. "Bloody hell. You made it hot enough!"

"Sorry, you want some cold water in it?" he asked, jumping up.

"It's okay. Coffee's meant to be hot, but... Sit down—no actual damage done. I can still talk," she replied with a smile.

The night progressed with both resting in armchairs in the lounge room near Toby. Every half hour, Ruby would check Toby. At six o'clock, the whimpers of Toby woke Charlie and Ruby, who had fallen asleep in their seats. Charlie, angry with himself for falling asleep, leapt up instantly. Ruby moved a little slower but came to Toby's side.

"G'day, mate," she said affectionately, taking Toby's head in her hands as she looked into his eyes. "Oh, there is someone in there! Welcome back."

Toby struggled to stand and fell back down. Ruby checked him over while Charlie stood close by, anxiously patting the dog's head. She turned to Charlie with a smile that lit her face. "I think he's gonna to be okay."

Again, Toby tried to stand as Ruby prepared another shot of a sedative to help Toby relax and give his system more time to recover.

"Ooh, I know what's like," Charlie said. "Don't worry, I won't let her do it too often."

Toby went limp and lay down without a fight. Ruby checked Toby before standing back, satisfied the dog would live. Charlie couldn't stop smiling.

"I could kiss you!" he exclaimed, ecstatically grabbing Ruby by the arms, dragging her into a hug. "Thank you! Thank you! Thank you."

Freeing herself from Charlie's embrace, she exclaimed, "Okay, settle down. He's going to be fine, but he needs to rest. He doesn't need you carrying on getting him all excited. Just calm."

Charlie took a step back.

"Sorry. You're right. Can I make you some breaky?"

The noise of Charlie's excitement aroused others trying to sleep off the punishment they'd put their bodies through the night before. As a few surfaced, Charlie felt the warmth of the morning sun thaw his stalled emotions.

More than breakfast, Ruby wanted a shower and to freshen up. Charlie grabbed a towel and showed her the way to the bathroom. As she showered, Charlie and Col got the barbeque going for a big fry-up breakfast. They decided to cook a feast: eggs, bacon, tomatoes, mushrooms, sausages, asparagus. Charlie wanted to celebrate. Pete took a quick trip to the local bakers to get fresh bread to go with the nosh-up.

By mid-morning, Ruby led Toby out to join the party. "He was hungry," she announced. "Not too much, Charlie. His system is still fragile. Maybe a bit of sausage only, or he might bring it back up."

Charlie would do anything she instructed. He had his mate back. He owed Ruby more than he could ever repay.

As they all sat outside on the deck enjoying the breakfast, Charlie and

Ruby found themselves separated from the group. As Charlie thanked her for the hundredth time, Ruby turned the conversation to something more constructive.

“Col told me he’s been encouraging you to become a consultant.”

“Yeah. He’s been like a dog with a bone. Ah,” he laughed, “appropriate analogy?”

“Terrible!” replied Ruby. “Are you thinking about it?”

“I don’t know. I have a pretty cushy job where I am. I know it. It’s not hard, usually, while still has its challenges. But ...”

“You like a bit of a challenge?”

“Yeah, maybe.”

“You should do it. What have you got to lose? You can always go back to your cushy job if it doesn’t work out. That’s how I see it, anyway.”

“Is that why you opened the practice?”

“Yeah. I enjoyed working at the zoo. The animals—and most of the humans—were good to work with. But my interest has always been farming and domestic animals. Something smaller than elephants.”

“What? Zebras are basically a horse, aren't they?”

“Mmm, no. Bit different. For one, they have stripes.”

They looked at each other and laughed.

“But I’ve seriously been nursing animals since I could walk! I grew up in the country. I know domestic animals. And I’ve done the study. So why not?”

“Fair enough. Not sure I have the business know-how or patience to learn.”

“Haha, it’s not that hard! You look like a well-organised person. That’s half the battle. And I can help you. I have time—unfortunately,” she said with a laugh. “Oh! I didn’t mean that... I mean, while I’m waiting for my clientele to build—"

Charlie laughed. “It’s okay. I know what you mean. No offence taken.”

He began to consider going out on his own. It was nothing new. Col had said the same to him and also offered to help. It could be a worthwhile move, he mused.

He sat looking at the breath of fresh air that had walked into his life. He put it down to lack of sleep but gave thanks for this woman who sat with him, glowing in the morning sun.

Chapter Fourteen

By lunchtime, most of the guests had left. The adrenalin had worn off and the sleepless night left both Charlie and Ruby needing sleep. After those left pitched in with the cleanup, Charlie finally got to bed. But he couldn't sleep. His mind was ticking over the events of the previous day. The anniversary was usually a tough day to get through and left him feeling alone and hollow. With the exception of Toby giving him a scare, for the first time in years he felt hopeful and wanted to plan for the future.

Over the following months, Charlie explored the idea of setting himself up as an environmental and agricultural consultant. The year had not been a good one for the grape growers of The Valley, and many tried-and-true practices were shown to be lacking. As Charlie and Col continued experimenting, other growers began coming to Charlie for advice. In the end, it was more by default than design that Charlie set up his own business.

By May, he had so much consulting work on his plate that he resigned from the secure government position to go solo. He had regular contact with Ruby, who was true to her word and helped set up the administration side of Charlie's business, acting sometimes as his personal administrative assistant.

"So. what's the story?" asked Pete one evening when he and Lucy met with Charlie for a meal.

"There is no story. She's been really helpful, that's all."

"Really helpful?" said Lucy. "Are you aware you haven't stopped talking about her all night?"

"She's right, Charlie. Ruby this, Ruby that. When are you gonna ask her out and not because you need help with emails?"

"I'm only asking cos she seems a big part of this consultancy thing," said Lucy.

Charlie said nothing. Had he been speaking continuously about Ruby? He wasn't sure.

"Charlie, you do know it's okay to think about ... a new relationship," Pete said tentatively.

"And where's it going to go? Nowhere. It's not like I can get married. And I'm not going to lead someone on."

"So, you have thought about it. You sly dog."

Charlie blushed. He couldn't explain to his friend the complication that he felt.

"It's not that easy, Simmo."

"Why?" asked Lucy innocently.

Charlie hesitated before replying. "Because of Myra."

"But she's gone."

Pete put a hand on Lucy's arm, aware she was treading on delicate territory.

"Sorry, Charlie," she began. "I don't mean to sound heartless, and I know it's hard for you, but are you to live a monk's life for the rest of your years? You're only thirty-five. That's a long time to be on your own. Don't you owe it to yourself to?"

"Enough, Lucy," said Pete, seeing the distress in his friend's eyes. "Charlie's a big boy. He can work it out for himself."

"I'm scared, Lucy," Charlie admitted, as he slumped against the table. He hadn't admitted that to himself before and was surprised when the words came out.

"What happened was a freak, Charlie. You can't live the rest of your life afraid of losing! Or you'll lose your whole life of potential joy with someone else!"

"It's not just about me. What can I offer someone? A fucked-up relationship with a man that's terrified of falling in love again. A man that can't offer a wedding and kids cos he's still legally married and can't get a divorce."

"Would you get a divorce if you could?" she asked.

Charlie thought about his response before saying, "I don't know."

"Really? After what she's put you through?" Lucy said, surprised.

"You didn't know her, Luce. She must have had her reasons."

"Yeah, I don't care. Those reasons are fucked up. And they've fucked you up, Charlie!"

Both men looked with raised eyebrows at this petite woman, telling it as she saw it.

"Charlie, you're hot. Sorry, Pete. You're a catch. You deserve so much more 'life' than you're allowing yourself. Don't let her ruin any more than she already has. You don't have to be married to be in a permanent relationship. And why shouldn't you have more kids?"

Charlie bristled. *No!* he thought. Losing Myra was devastating, but he couldn't bear the thought of losing another child.

"I can't go there again," he replied. "That's ... too much."

"Then you're going to become a very lonely man, Charlie."

"I'm getting used to that," he replied with a snigger.

Charlie went home with the words of Lucy ringing in his ears. She was right. Having Toby in his life had made a difference. But it wasn't the same as having a partner in life. For as long as he could remember, he wanted to have a family. After the tragedy, he'd abandoned that–or thought he had. He had clearly set himself up for the solitary life, but deep down the yearning to be a part of a family unit still called. He wanted to feel 'complete' again but was afraid.

He could feel the anger rising toward Myra. He would never understand why she did what she did. Where was she now? Leading a happy life somewhere, most likely. She'd moved on, so why couldn't he? The feeling of sympathy accompanied the anger he felt. On the one hand, he could never forgive her. On the other, if she were to show up, he would probably be filled with compassion for her.

His thoughts turned to Ruby. She embodied everything Myra did not. She was the country girl, happy to play backyard cricket, get dirty, sit up all night with an animal. She had ambitions, but they revolved around a country practice, not seeing it as a stepping-stone to a city practice. She liked the house being on the banks of the river. If he'd met Ruby years ago, he would have jumped at the opportunity of a relationship. But now ...

He realised he had been acting selfishly while believing he was protecting her. Asking Ruby to help with the business set-up as often as he had, he realised had ulterior motives. He didn't want to lead her on or hurt her. She deserved so much more than that. So he resolved to take a step back; distance himself so she didn't get hurt.

Charlie walked outside to Issie's garden. The late autumn evening was cold and damp. Toby raised himself from his warm bed to join his master in the yard. He went straight to the tree and cocked his leg. Charlie watched and realised how big and strong the tree had become. Strong enough to hang the swing he'd always planned to put there. His thoughts invariably turned to Isabella, who would have been about three and a half. Too small still to swing on her own, he thought, but would no doubt have loved it. He envisioned her sitting, calling for someone to come and push her while he worked around the yard. The thought made him sad yet smile. This would be a pleasure he'd never get to experience. There would be no more children for him. Of that, he was sure.

The sudden chilly wind startled him, pulling him out of his melancholy. He could see Isabella as a precocious three-year-old stamping her feet, demanding something. What she wanted; he didn't know. But she was telling him something.

"Sorry, Issie, I'm not sure what you're saying," he said aloud.

He turned to go back inside, chilled by the sudden rush of wind. Calling Toby, they walked back to the house. The feeling he had when he stood by Isabella's grave on the first anniversary of the incident came to him. He thought she'd made it known then that she didn't want him to live in the land with the dead but to get on with living. Now, as he walked toward the house that represented his new beginning, the feeling returned. His daughter was giving him the kick in the butt that he needed to keep moving forward.

"It won't be easy, though, Issie. I miss you."

There was no reply.

If he were to move on, he had to try again to find Myra, if for no reason other than to get a divorce. He didn't want to be an island for the rest of his life. He didn't know what, if anything, he had to offer someone, but he didn't want to be alone.

¥

The next day, Charlie went to see the police sergeant, Phil Cook. He would again search for Myra. This time, Cookie seemed a little more willing to help. He agreed to speak with the officers who had found Myra and at least try to get a message to her. See if she was willing to have contact yet. If not, Cookie knew a private investigator Charlie could approach who could help without the restrictions that the police force placed on him.

Charlie kept himself busy with work as Cookie made enquiries.

Busily working in his shed, he heard a vehicle pull into his driveway. He was a little surprised as Ruby got out of the car. He hadn't seen her and had barely spoken to her for several months. Charlie had followed through on his decision and consciously distanced himself from her. She was young and had a lifetime of experiences to be had. She didn't need him and all the baggage he brought with him, tying her down, he'd told himself.

As she walked toward the house, Charlie called her towards the shed. Toby appeared excitedly to welcome her, barking and jumping around her making it difficult to walk in a straight line.

"Well, someone's pleased to see me," she said, as she reached the shed.

Charlie smiled and waved. Ruby talked as if nothing had changed while Charlie remained withdrawn, giving minimal answers to questions. He explained his absence on the amount of work piled up on his desk. Ruby nodded, acknowledging that work could be demanding.

Silence fell between them. Charlie persisted with being aloof while Ruby wriggled uneasily. Finally, she summoned the courage to say what she'd come to say.

"Charlie, have I done something?" she asked.

"What do you mean?"

"Well, I thought we were friends, then suddenly you disappeared and I haven't heard from you for months."

"Yes, you have. I spoke to you only the other day."

“That was two weeks ago, Charlie, and only because I called you. In fact, had I not been the one making the phone calls, I doubt we would have spoken at all in the last three months. Even then you didn’t seem to be able to get off the phone quick enough. What’s going on?”

Charlie stopped what he was doing and turned to her.

“You’re right. I’m sorry. There it is again! I’m forever saying ‘sorry’ to you,” he said, making light of the moment. Ruby, however, didn’t laugh.

“I’m not sure what you want me to say. Work has been busy.”

“Work’s always been busy, Charlie, but it didn’t stop you from calling me late at night when you had a spare minute. What’s changed? Is it me? Is it something I said?”

“No! Ruby, it’s not you.”

“Then what?” she hesitated before continuing. “I really like you, Charlie, and I thought ... I thought you liked me, too.”

She looked sheepish, and Charlie felt like the cad he was. He kept away so she didn’t get hurt. Yet here she stood, confused and hurt.

“Ruby, I like you, too. But you’re young and have your whole life ahead of you. You don’t need me weighing you down.”

"My god, you're talking as if you're twice my age! Charlie, you're seven years older than me. Yes, you've had some pretty shit stuff to deal with. I get that. But don't you also still have your whole life ahead of you?"

"Ruby, I don't want to lead you on. You can do better than me."

"I'm talking about a friendship, Charlie. I haven't asked you to marry me!"

"Just as well, cos I couldn't."

"Charlie, stop. I know your story. What you haven't told me, others have. I miss you, Charlie. I thought we were mates."

"And you're telling me that's it?" he asked. "You only see me as a mate? You wouldn't want more?"

"I'd be lying if I said that. I really like you, Charlie. You have your limitations and I have mine. But we were good–as friends. If that's all you can give, that's fine. I can live with that. Just don't shut me out. And I miss Toby."

"Toby?" he said, suddenly smiling.

"Yeah. A special bond grew between us after the snake bite," she said, coyly.

"Ahahahaha," he bellowed. "And who am I to stand between you two?"

Ruby moved to stand in front of Charlie. They looked into each other's eyes and Charlie felt the warmth of this woman standing before him filling his senses.

"I've missed you, too," he said. "But you need to know I'm damaged goods."

"I know you are. I just want my friend back."

"Well, you know what they say."

Ruby looked at him perplexed.

"Toby and me are a package deal. You can't have him as your friend without me," he said with a cheeky smile.

Ruby laughed. "Well, if I can have my mate back, I'm sure I can at least tolerate his master," she replied.

Charlie took Ruby in his arms and hugged her.

"Sorry," he said.

She returned the hug with equal amounts of warmth. Charlie allowed himself to stop thinking and live in the moment for the first time in years. Here was this beautiful young woman standing before him. Realising how much he'd missed her, he didn't want to shut himself off from her any longer. No more living in the past. He had to take a chance, allow himself to feel some happiness and see where it led.

Chapter Fifteen

Charlie looked for excuses to call Ruby: a business request, questions about Toby's diet, whatever he could conjure up. Slowly, their friendship grew. Charlie told Ruby about Myra, Issie G and the incident. He told her of Myra's choice to leave and not have contact with him, how it had broken his heart and disturbed him beyond his ability to express. He spoke of his fears for the future and what he could and couldn't offer anyone. All the while, Ruby sat undisturbed, taking it in.

"It sounds to me," she said, "like you're overthinking and talking yourself out of moving forward."

Charlie stared at her in confusion before responding. "I don't think you're right. I'm just putting my cards on the table, so, you know ..."

"So you don't get hurt, she said. "Charlie, how about we take one step at a time? Not twelve!"

She was right, Charlie knew. But he didn't want Ruby, or any woman, thinking he could offer a 'happy ever after' type of relationship. He couldn't offer a family. He couldn't even offer marriage! Ruby was young and could attract any man in The Valley. If she had ambitions of one day having a family, she should not waste her time on him.

"I like you and I think you like me. I understand you're scared, but let's hang out and see where this goes. You don't have to look for excuses to call me, either," she said with a grin. "We'll cross other bridges as they come. Okay?"

The friendship between Charlie and Ruby was effortless. With a shared interest in so many things, it wasn't difficult to be around each other. Despite Charlie telling himself to take his time, his actions betrayed a sense of urgency.

Several months passed. They sat on the back deck drinking their Jack Daniels with the gas heater pumping and blankets around them to ward off the winter cold. Steam could be seen coming from their mouths and noses in the glow from the heater as they spoke.

Feelings of 'like' grew stronger, but Charlie struggled to say the words. His fear of ruining Ruby's life remained strong.

"I'm not thinking about kids, Charlie. My focus is on the practice at the moment and getting that up and running well. I don't need the complication."

"But you will one day."

She thought for a moment before saying, "Maybe. Or maybe not. They're not the be-all and end-all for me."

They sat in silence again. Charlie considered his fears, as Ruby envisioned a life together. Charlie's thoughts, as they so often did, returned to Myra. Thinking about his wife while comfortably seated with another woman was odd. But, for a change, he didn't feel like he was being unfaithful. He had lost all genuine feelings for Myra. Looking at the woman next to him, he smiled. He didn't want to scare her away and desperately wanted to give a romantic relationship a go. Instinct took over as Charlie took Ruby in his arms and kissed her passionately. She melted into his body returning the feelings. He felt a level of passion and he hadn't felt for a long time. He wanted her with Ruby's response mirroring him.

Nevertheless, a persistent voice continued to nag. Regardless of what Myra wanted, he still couldn't move on entirely while married to her. She had what she wanted, which was nothing to do with Charlie. Perhaps it was time for him to demand what he needed from her. If she didn't want to be his wife or in his life, then she needed to finalise that with a divorce.

As the lingering kiss ended, Charlie pulled back. "There's something else you need to know," he said, taking Ruby's hand.

"What?"

"I decided I'm going to try again to find Myra."

Ruby squirmed in the seat, moving away from Charlie. She stared at him for further explanation as Charlie gazed into the distance over the river and to the hill on the far side. Ruby removed her hand from his as she waited for him to share what he was thinking.

"I can't," he began, struggling to find the words, "I can't move on knowing she's out there somewhere and we're still legally tied."

"Do you still love her?"

"Do I love her?" Charlie repeated, thinking about his answer. "Do I love her? I don't think so."

"But you're not sure? Is that why you want to find her?" Ruby asked, her voice as fragile as she felt.

"No. She made her choice. She left with no explanation. Made it clear she doesn't want to be in my life. I won't pretend to understand that, but that's how it is."

"Then why find her?"

"For closure."

Charlie suddenly realised the impact of his declaration on the new woman in his life. Turning to look at her, he saw the anguish in her eyes. Feeling like a heel, he sat to face her. Placing one arm around her shoulders and taking her hand in his, he tried to explain.

"Rubes, this has little to do with 'us'. Well, it does, but it doesn't. Regardless of 'us', I need to find her. Not because I still care. If anything, I'd probably rip her head off for what she did. I would like an explanation, but doubt I'll get one. The important thing, for me, for closure is to get a divorce. No offence, but I'm in no hurry to remarry. In fact, I can't see that in my future. But I feel that while I'm still married to Myra, I can't be 100% free of her. It's been over three years. If she were going to come back, she would have by now. She's not a part of my life. She's not apart of our daughter's ... I bet she doesn't even know where Isabella's buried. She means very little to me now. But she's still my wife.

I want her out of my life officially. The connection broke a long time ago. I feel trapped by her."

Ruby nodded her understanding. "I get it. I do. But I can't pretend that it will be easy for me. If that will help you put the past behind you, then do it."

the two sat amicably as Ruby asked, how Charlie would go about it. He wasn't sure. Having tried before without success. He would hire someone, a professional PI, to help.

"I don't have to see her, you know. We can get a divorce without seeing each other."

"You have to see her, Charlie."

"No, I–"

"Yes! Yes, Charlie, you do! You deserve explanations, or you'll spend the rest of your life wondering. You need to see her and have a conversation. As you've said, there's a good chance she won't want to. But for your peace of mind, you need to try."

Again, she was right, of course. This woman was turning out to understand him better than he understood himself. Charlie pulled her to him, holding her affectionately.

"Thank you," he said, kissing her forehead.

Ruby said nothing in return. She couldn't. She felt a small stab in her heart that she couldn't show him. It wouldn't be fair to this man who was still trying to get his life back in order three years after an ordeal no one should have to endure. She vowed to support him as best she could no matter how testing this would be for her. She held him tightly, burying her head against his chest.

¥

Charlie found and hired a private investigator with the help of Cookie and Simmo. While the PI went finding Myra, Charlie tried not to over think what would happen when she was found.

Charlie and Ruby seemed inseparable. Before long, a portion of the work shed became a makeshift menagerie as Ruby brought some of the animals she nursed along for weekend stays with Charlie.

Life felt the best it had been in years for Charlie. He still regularly sat in Issie's garden and talked to his daughter and often took Ruby with him and she would talk to Issie, usually recounting a funny story about Charlie. They appeared like any other young couple in love; frequenting restaurants and bars, accepting invitations as a couple and planning weekends away.

Charlie was grateful to have this amazing woman in his life. She had brought the sunshine and warmth he'd been missing. But still Myra would creep into his thoughts. She sat as the dark cloud hovering on the horizon, threatening to end the beautiful new day.

It had been three months and Tom, the private investigator, had found nothing. Charlie wondered if he had hired the right man on the job. How could she just disappear—again?

"She could have moved overseas," Tom had explained. "She could have changed her name."

"But surely there's a public record of people that change their names."

"No. Not necessarily. It's a bit of a 'need to know' basis. Official institutions like the bank."

"That's ridiculous."

"Not really, Charlie."

"So I have to spend the rest of my life married to a woman that no longer exists. Great!"

"You can apply for a divorce, Charlie. It's not easy, but it can be done."

The thought had never occurred to Charlie. Vaguely he remembered Lucy advising him of this. Suddenly, the thought confused him, confronted with this possibility. Did he honestly want a divorce? He loved Ruby and saw them living out a life together. Questioning his thoughts both shocked and revolted him. After all she'd put him through, did he still have feelings of affection for his wife?

Charlie left the PI feeling heavy. What should he do? He decided nothing. He'd give Tom a little longer to find Myra. There was no hurry to decide. Did he have no desire to remarry? Or did he only want to be married to Myra?

Arriving back at the block, Ruby sat in the garden. Charlie was surprised, expecting her to be still working somewhere in The Valley. He pulled his thoughts away from Myra as he got out of the car. She turned and smiled at him. His heart melted a little at the love and warmth that looked back at him. Ruby was perfect, he reminded himself.

Ruby walked toward him, a calming influence on his troubled mind.

"Well, this is a nice surprise, Rusty! Thought you'd be off checking a lame duck or something," he said, laughing.

"Careful!" she said. "I do more than ducks. Progressed to chickens as well."

"Haha. That's my girl."

Charlie placed an arm around her shoulder and kissed her head as they walked toward the house. "So, what are you doing here so early?"

Without hesitating, Ruby replied. "Came to see how the investigation was going. Thought you might need some company. You know, checking up on you."

"Thanks. I'm okay, though" he lied. "And no news. She's done a great job of disappearing!"

"Could she be overseas?"

"That's what Tom wondered."

"You going to keep trying?"

"What choice do I have?"

"And what happens if you find her? What will you do then? If it's just about a divorce, there are other options."

"Mmm."

"What does 'mmm' mean?" she asked.

Charlie said nothing. How could he tell this wonderful creature that she was right? That he wanted to see his wife, that he needed to find her and talk to her? Instead of replying, he stopped and kissed her passionately before taking her hand and leading her towards the house.

"Don't dismiss me, Charlie. What's going on in your head?"

Charlie went straight through the house, grabbing a beer on the way, to his favourite spot on the back deck overlooking the river before he tried to answer. Taking a deep breath, he shrugged his shoulders.

"What can I say? I thought it was just for a divorce. But I don't think it is. I need to find her and talk to her."

Ruby reached for the railing, choosing to watch the river rather than let her eyes show the hurt she felt. She attempted to be supportive and understanding, but the deeper her love for him became, the harder it became to distance herself emotionally.

Guessing some of her thoughts, Charlie moved behind her and wrapped his arms around her.

"This has nothing to do with you or us, you know. I love you," he said, kissing her head and gripping her.

"Myra may have nothing to do with me, but Charlie, don't you see? She's sitting smack bang in the middle of this relationship. I want you to find peace and if that means finding Myra, so be it. I just wonder sometimes if ..."

"If what?"

"If maybe you're still in love with her."

Charlie took a step back and looked unwaveringly into Ruby's eyes.

"I told you this relationship wasn't going to be easy. To have so many questions left unanswered is hard. I'm scared, Rubes, constantly scared. Scared I'm going to lose you, scared of finding Myra, scared of not finding Myra. I'm sorry I can't be any more than I am. But don't doubt my love for you. In fact, I've been thinking."

"What, Charlie?"

"Why don't you move in? We're pretty much living together between the two houses. Why not save ourselves some money and you move in here?"

Ruby looked at Charlie. He seemed genuine, but was he ready for her to move in?

"I wouldn't say it if I didn't mean it, Rubes. You should know that by now."

Ruby pulled the man before her into her arms, nestling her head on his shoulder.

"I'd like that, Charlie. But only if you're ready."

"I'm as ready as I'll ever be," he said.

The truth of the statement not missing either of them.

The decision was made. Within thirty minutes, Charlie had gone from thinking about what he would do if he found his wife to moving in with his new love. He didn't know if he was doing the right thing but had to keep putting one foot in front of the other, he told himself.

Chapter Sixteen

Ruby moved in as summer approached. Charlie made space for her and the animals that came with her with another shed was being constructed to act as an animal hospital. While Ruby's primary practice remained in the town, the business had grown to a point where she could take on another veterinarian. And, as Charlie made room for Ruby at the block, Ruby made space for Charlie to have an office for his consulting business at the practice in town.

This year, Charlie decided not to hold a gathering on the anniversary. Instead, he and Ruby went on a holiday. They headed to Tasmania and Cradle Mountain. Here, they walked and explored the beauty of the Cradle Mountain-Lake St Clair National Park. They climbed to the summit, picnicked by Dove Lake, and enjoyed ten days in the fresh air.

On their return, life seemed busier than ever. The new year brought more contracts for Charlie. Ruby was inundated with racehorses requiring attention after an exceptionally bad racing season.

Charlie kept in touch with Tom, the private investigator, but he still had few leads. It had been months and Tom was certain Myra was no longer in the country. Charlie had spent a small fortune attempting to track her down but drew the line at beginning the search overseas. Myra could be anywhere. She had spoken many times in the earlier part of their relationship about living and working in London. She may have finally followed through with that plan. However, she had also spoken of living and working in Geneva. He couldn't afford to ask Tom to track through Europe in the slim hope he may find the woman.

Tom had suggested several times to drop the search and forget about her. But Charlie couldn't. Ruby, knowing Charlie's unease, had done some homework, too. She'd found out how he could get a divorce without her, but Charlie wasn't interested, reinstating it was about more than just a divorce.

For Ruby, it felt like the twist of a dagger in her heart. She didn't care about getting married. She was happy to spend her life as they were, as long as they were together. But his resistance to getting a divorce without Myra's consent and cooperation disquieted her. His reasoning behind finding Myra seemed to change regularly. It was to start divorce proceedings, to get answers, to tell her how she'd destroyed his life. She was sure he was still holding out some hope for Myra, regardless of what he said, but wasn't sure. All she could do was quietly support him in his turmoil.

Autumn arrived and with it came unusually cold winds. Ruby fell ill and remained ill for longer, than normal. Whatever was ailing her kept her constantly tired and run down, unable to shake it. After a month, she became concerned about her health and went to see her doctor. She'd clashed with Charlie frequently, maintaining that it was the flu. However, Charlie remained unconvinced. He was sure something more was wrong and insisted she have a check-up. Charlie said he'd take her, but she was adamant he would not be going with her if she saw a doctor. The last thing she needed was him talking to the doctor as if Ruby was about to die. His exaggerated concern touched her, but she feared her suffering wasn't life-threatening, but would rock Charlie's world.

When Ruby returned from the doctor, Charlie waited in an agitated state in the kitchen. He had convinced himself that it was something serious. What would he do if she had cancer? Or if she needed expensive medical treatment? He struggled to compose himself and avoid overthinking but found it challenging. Fear being a constant companion, it was the immediate response to anything out of the ordinary. He didn't want to think about what he'd do if anything happened to Ruby.

He rushed to the front door as Ruby entered, took her handbag and coat and placing them on the hallstand before leading her into the lounge room.

"Oh, Charlie, stop! I'm not dying!" she exclaimed as he carefully helped her sit.

“You’re okay then?” he asked, somewhat surprised.

“I’m okay,” she replied hesitantly. "I told you it would pass."

“But ... you’ve been so ill. You’ve been working too hard? Is that it?” he asked.

“Charlie, sit down.”

Charlie did as he was instructed.

“There is something and I don’t know how to tell you, so, I’m just going to say it.”

Charlie waited, staring at her curiously.

“Charlie,” Ruby couldn’t look at him. “I’m pregnant.”

The silence in the room was deafening. Charlie stood and moved to the window without saying a word.

“Aren’t you going to say something?”

“How did this happen?”

“Really? I think we both know how–”

“Don’t, Ruby.”

“Well, what do you mean ‘how did this happen’?”

“I told you I didn’t want kids. I can’t ...”

“Charlie, I didn’t plan this. But it’s happened.”

“I can’t–”

“What happened with Issie was a terrible, freaky accident!”

“You don’t know!” he said, raising his voice. “You don’t know what it’s like to love someone so much and then have them taken away from you. I can’t go through that again.”

“Who says you’re going to have to? Charlie, this baby will probably live to be 100–long after you've gone," Ruby rambled. The fear Charlie carried with him always left her struggling for words.

"Charlie, I've thought about this," she said in a hushed voice, "if you want, I will terminate."

Charlie spun around to look at her.

"We don't have to have it. If it's too much for you ... I love you, Charlie, and as long as I have you in my life, I have all I need. The choice is yours."

Ruby stood from the couch and left the room, leaving Charlie to contemplate what he wanted. Her heart was heavy at the thought of what he would decide. Although she didn't want to lose the baby, she was willing to do it for him. She would do anything for him. She knew enough of the pain he had endured to realise she couldn't ask any more of him. That she had him at all was a miracle. And, as she contemplated losing the life of the thing growing inside her, she realised just how intense his pain must have been. Ruby lay on the bed and cried silent tears, distancing herself from the life she carried and the choice she'd given away.

Charlie stood at the window in the lounge room, unmoved. He stared out at the cloud forming over the mountain. The rain would be here soon, he thought. He watched the wind whip through the trees and the dust rise from the driveway. Charlie turned and headed for the front door. Grabbing his coat, he headed out wishing the wind could clear his head.

He had been so sure Ruby would come home with news of a disease. He had been bracing himself, preparing to hear she was going to be fighting for her life. At no point had he thought of her being pregnant. He now recognised the foolishness of his thoughts. Of course she was pregnant. All the signs were there. He'd made it clear that this was not something he ever wanted again, and all but convinced himself it couldn't happen.

Charlie could feel himself getting angry. How could she do this to him? What was it with these women that played with his emotions so recklessly? He was sick of it, sick of being treated like his feelings didn't count, what he wanted didn't count. Sick of being the victim in their games.

The weather continued to deteriorate as Charlie pounded his way through the bush track. He came to the dark and menacing clearing where the swimming hole once, not realising how far he'd walked or in what direction he'd gone. Huffing and puffing from the effort, he sat on a boulder, thinking about the last time he'd been here. It had been years since he'd sat on the same boulder, coming to terms with the loss of his wife and daughter. Now he sat coming to terms with a new life on its way.

His anger seemed to get blown away by the wind as he sat thinking about Ruby. He remembered weeks earlier that he'd been the one, not Ruby, to act instinctively. She protested. Not the other way around. And now she offered to end the pregnancy if he didn't want to keep the baby. How self-righteous, condescending and wrong he'd been.

He softened at the thought of Ruby lying in their bed at home, probably feeling some of what he'd felt when he lost Isabella.

Charlie felt a complete heel and got up to rush back to her side. How could he have been so callous? He automatically thought he was the victim again. When, in actual fact, Ruby was the victim. She'd given up all hopes of marriage for him, prepared to be childless for him. And now that she'd fallen pregnant because of his mistake, she was willing to surrender the child for him. He couldn't ask her to do that. As painful as it may be for him to welcome another child into his life, it was the least he could do for Ruby if she wanted to keep it.

Charlie rushed home as quickly as he could. The rain had arrived and hampered his return, sometimes blinding him and making the path perilously slippery. When he got to the house, he bounded to the bedroom.

Ruby jumped up in surprise, hearing the commotion coming in the door. Charlie was dripping, making puddles on the floor.

"Are you alright?" she asked, as his distressed form moved closer.

"Rubes, I'm so sorry," he began, plonking himself on the bed. He took her hand and looked apologetically at her. "I'm so sorry. I have been utterly selfish and you ... you have been nothing but giving and giving to me since day one."

Ruby gazed at the man she loved, unsure what to make of his statement.

"What are you saying, Charlie?" she asked.

"You're pregnant because of me."

"Well, der..."

"No, I mean, I'm the one who insisted, a month or so back."

"Again, der!"

"But you said nothing. You didn't attack me, remind me, confront me ... nothing. You just said you'd get rid of it if I wanted you to."

"If that's what you want, Charlie." Ruby's pale face defied the inner torment she felt.

"I've already taken a lot from you and put a lot on you. I can't ask you to do that for me. If you want to keep it, so do I."

Ruby could no longer maintain the stoic facade. She quietly put her arms around him and cried. "Thank you, Charlie. Thank you! I didn't know how I was going to bring myself to terminate. The thought repulses me. But–"

"But you would have for me. Oh Ruby, I'm sorry for putting you in that position. What did I do to deserve you?"

The pair cried, and held each other as realisation sunk in. They were going to having a baby. Both were as anxious as each other at what that would mean.

"I'd better hurry and find Myra, I think," stated Charlie.

"Myra? Why?" asked Ruby, surprised that once again another woman sat between her and her man.

"To make an honest woman of you. If we're going to be a family–"

“Charlie, I thought we already were a family.”

The disappointment in her eyes wasn't lost on Charlie.

“We are,” he corrected himself. "Of course we are."

“This is our moment, Charlie, not hers. For once, can we leave her out of this conversation?”

Charlie looked away, regretting bringing Myra up. If only he could leave her behind, he thought.

Chapter Seventeen

They had made the decision. Charlie couldn't go back on it now, but he continued to have mixed feelings. Over the previous four and a half years, he'd imagined the life for his dead daughter. She would be in kindergarten now had she lived. All the things he'd imagined doing with his child—fishing, camping, bonfires—he imagined doing with her. While she may not be around, she lived on in his memory and imagination. Now, that imagined relationship was to be shattered by a real, live human being. And who was to say this one wouldn't leave him as Issie had done? How could he bring himself to love another child, especially if it was a girl?

He tried not to dwell on the thought. Ruby, in amongst the morning sickness, seemed happy about having a baby. As always, she was gentle with him and waited for him to catch up with her. But she wouldn't deny the child she carried and would love it enough for both of them until Charlie could let go of fear and love the child himself.

Charlie had stepped up contact with Tom, the private investigator. He was hell-bent on finding Myra now. He wasn't always sure why, other than he still needed closure. How could he begin a new life with a new family while part of his old family still walked about officially connected to him?

But all roads seemed blocked, and Tom was losing patience. He had no more avenues to explore. He suggested to Charlie to find another PI that may have a fresh approach, but Charlie saw that as a backward step. He'd already invested so much in Tom that he didn't want to return to the beginning and start again.

Charlie hid his feelings as much as possible and acted as best he could. He sensed a tension between himself and Ruby, unsure if it was genuine. Now and then, she asked about the investigation and query why he was persisting. Her questions didn't appear to be out of any malice or bad feeling, but Charlie couldn't help wondering if she resented him. He'd been looking for Myra for so long now that it was like a habit and he wasn't sure why anymore. It had almost become an addiction that he couldn't give up.

"There's plenty of time to worry about that," he would say each time Ruby raised arrangements for the new child.

At eighteen weeks, when it was time for an ultrasound scan, he proclaimed that he could not make it as he had meetings with clients. Ruby offered alternate dates and times and even asked him to find something that did suit him, to no avail. Every scan and obstetric appointment was met with the same response.

"Charlie, you can't keep doing this, you know," she said as gently as she could, hiding her frustration.

Charlie played dumb, saying he didn't know what she was talking about.

"Look at me, Charlie. Feel my belly. Your child is in there! You said you wanted it. But other than those words a few months ago, you've done very little to show me they are true. It's too late now. I'm having this baby! So, are you going to be a part of it? Or not?"

Charlie hated it when she was so succinct and left him no room to move. And, of course, she was right. He thought he had agreed to it. He had to come to terms with this new creature that would be in his world in no time.

"Maybe I can move some meetings around and fit it in at 4.00 p.m. on Monday," he replied.

Maybe if he saw the baby on the monitor, it would help him come to terms with it. He thought about when he first saw Isabella on the monitor and it had blown his mind. The bump was a real, live human being growing in Myra. He'd fallen instantly in love with his unborn child. He hoped seeing this one would be as wondrous and life-changing, but he doubted it.

"They'll ask if we want to know the sex."

After thinking for a minute, he replied, "Does it matter?"

"I don't know, Charlie. Does it?" replied Ruby accusingly.

"No, not to me. But if you'd like to know, I'm happy with that."

"Let's see how we feel on Monday," said Ruby, ending the conversation.

¥

Monday and the time for the scan came around sooner than Charlie was ready for. As they sat in the clinic awaiting their turn, they exchanged few words. Ruby sat reading a four-month-old copy of a woman's magazine while Charlie looked around the waiting room. Pictures of babies seemed to haunt him. The palms of his hands grew sweaty as he waited what felt like a lifetime for Ruby's name to be called.

Finally, their turn arrived.

"You okay?" Ruby asked.

"Sure!" Charlie replied, unconvincingly. "Let's go see the shadow."

"The shadow? That's not a nice thing to call him ... or her."

"When you see the ultrasound, you'll understand," he said, laughing at his joking comment.

In no time, the radiographer presented an image on the screen. A fuzzy grey and white image appeared as the doctor announced it was their baby. Charlie looked, feeling nothing but terror, while Ruby looked in wonder.

"I can't quite–" she began.

"These images are always hard to see," said Charlie. "Doc, can you do that 3D thing? Makes it easier to see the outline."

"Yes, just give me a minute or two longer here. I need to take some measurements," the doctor replied leisurely.

"Okay. Here we go," he said as the image on the screen changed.

Ruby gasped as the image of their baby became clearer. Charlie made a silly comment about the sepia colour being undervalued these days, but no one else seemed to find it funny.

"Hello, little one!" Ruby exclaimed, talking to the monitor. "I'm your Mum. Aren't you gorgeous!"

"Gorgeous? It looks little more than a blob to me," said Charlie.

The radiographer turned to Charlie and raised her eyebrows, surprised at the comment. Charlie immediately apologised.

"Don't mind your dad," said Ruby. "He's got some issues. I promise to love you until he sorts himself out."

"Steady!" said Charlie.

"Are you going to deny it?" Ruby challenged.

"No. I guess not."

Charlie looked again at the image on the screen that seemed to wave. His heart was being pulled from his chest as he looked. The memories of when he first saw Issie came flooding back. The pain of losing her. It was overwhelming. He couldn't do this.

"Sorry, Rubes," he said before leaving the room.

He walked quickly through the reception area and out the front door. Charlie stood in the car park in the cool drizzle of the early winter evening. Suddenly, he threw up. How could he do this? He didn't want to let Ruby down but couldn't find the strength to stay beside her. From within, a voice whispered, acknowledging his old dream of having a wife and children. While he thought the dream had long since died, he heard the faint call of recognition that the dream wasn't dead. He wanted a family. He wanted children. And he wanted them with Ruby. So why was he finding it all so hard?

A few minutes later, Ruby came out of the clinic. Silently, they went to the car.

"Sorry–"

"Don't, Charlie," she said, cutting him short.

They drove without talking for some time before Ruby broke the silence.

"This isn't going to work, Charlie," she began. "You said you were on board with this. Need I remind you this result is of your choosing! But, once again, I feel like I'm the one paying the price for it. You have turned my life upside down, Charlie. You need to decide whether or not you really are a part of it."

"Rubes, I am–"

"I don't want words, Charlie! Prove it to me. Cos, if you're not, that's fine. I'll raise our daughter on my own."

"Daughter?" Charlie asked.

Ruby hesitated before replying. "Yes, Charlie. I decided I wanted to know. I didn't think you cared either way, but if it was a girl–you may need time to get your head around it if you are going to be a part of our lives. Isabella has a sister."

They continued in silence for some time before Ruby tried again.

"You have to decide, Charlie. I can't continue like this. You say one thing and do another."

"That's a bit unfair!" Charlie protested.

"Is it? I feel like I'm always playing second fiddle to Myra, even though you say you love me and not her. You helped make this baby. You said you wouldn't ask me to sacrifice any more than I already have for this relationship, but it's all words, Charlie. It's me and a future with our daughter, or I'll go it alone. You choose."

The words stung. Everything Charlie feared most was before him again. Not in the same form they had been last time, but he was about to lose everything for a second time if he wasn't careful.

"I don't want to lose you, Ruby."

"And the baby?"

Charlie hesitated. "I don't want to lose her either. I truly don't. I'm just ... I don't know."

"Then find out, Charlie! This has to stop. This baby deserves better than this. And so do I."

Ruby's words had stung. While Charlie wanted to blame pregnancy hormones for her harsh tones, he couldn't. She was justified in her anger.

Charlie would inform Tom he would end the search. Wherever Myra was, she could stay lost. As difficult as it was to walk away, he had to show Ruby he was trying.

¥

Isabella would have been turning five and to celebrate, Charlie made an addition to her garden. Taking Ruby by the hand, he led her outside, insisting she keep her eyes closed.

"What are you doing, Charlie? It's freezing out here!" she protested.

"You'll see," was all he would say until they reached the garden.

"Okay, open your eyes," he instructed.

Ruby opened her eyes and looked around, bewildered.

"What am I looking at?" she asked.

"The lights," he replied simply.

"The lights?"

"Yes! How is she going to play in the garden in the dark?"

"Who?" asked Ruby, baffled.

"You know what today is?"

"Yes, Issie G's birthday. So, you've put lights in the garden for her? Charlie, you're scaring me."

"Not for her!" he said, exasperated. "For her," he said, pointing at Ruby's stomach. "How can she come play in the garden without lights?"

"You put lights in Issie's garden on Issie's birthday for ... Missy?" asked Ruby as realisation dawned.

With a sense of relief, Charlie exclaimed, "Yes!"

Ruby looked at Charlie. Filled with love and wonder, she said, "I love you, Charlie."

"I'm trying Rubes."

"Yes, you are! Bloody trying!"

"Ah, ah, now. Language in front of the children."

Ruby put her arms around Charlie. Thank you was all she could manage. This man would continue to confound and surprise her every step of the way.

Chapter Eighteen

The late spring evening seemed biting as she drove through the misty valley. She'd planned on arriving much earlier than this, but the delayed flight had set her back. She drove down the once familiar street, a little unsure of what she would do or say.

She'd booked a nearby hotel; however, with time to kill, she drove toward Powelltown and passed the hamlet she had called home for a short time, Gilderoy. As she neared the block, she slowed. To her surprise, she saw a new house occupying the once familiar block. What had she expected? That time would stand still after she left.

For Myra, time stood still for a long time. Her departure left her hating herself and everything connected to that day. She'd wanted to come back. She'd wanted to explain. But she just couldn't. Instead, she fled as far away as she could manage. For the best part of five years, she'd been running. She was tired. It had to stop and she knew the only way that could happen was by coming back and facing the past.

As Myra pulled the car to a stop at the side of the road a safe distance from the house, she could make out two people in the yard. They were too distant to discern, but one had the posture and gait of Charlie, she thought, and the other looked like a pregnant woman. She felt a twinge of something as she watched them, hand in hand, move toward the house. Several trees and shrubs soon hindered her line of sight. The block looked good; the house lovely and the garden expansive. It had the feel of Charlie and she smiled.

Was she ready to knock on the front door and face him? She didn't think so. What if it wasn't him? Her plan wasn't very well thought out. She knew she had to see Charlie and offer some explanation but had few expectations. He had clearly moved on if that had been Charlie in the front yard.

The twinge she felt she recognised as envy. The incident many years ago had left her feeling almost nothing. She'd travelled from place to place, never really connecting with anyone or experiencing love. Fear held her back. She didn't trust herself enough to commit to another. She didn't want to hurt anyone else the way she knew she had hurt Charlie. Yet she longed to feel comfort again, to feel she belonged somewhere.

As Myra started the car and drove up the road toward Powelltown, she wondered if she really had belonged there. She'd always thought that had been part of the problem. She was an outsider and would always be an outsider in everyone else's eyes. She'd made friends and people accepted Charlie's choice of woman, but she never really belonged.

Myra stopped outside the combined Powellie Pub and General Store to turn the car around. As she did, she saw Cookie and another local policeman. Cookie walked into the store while the other man walked towards the police car. He looked her way with a quizzical expression. You could always see the cogs turning with the local policeman, she thought. She took off as quickly as possible. She wanted time to prepare herself for seeing and talking to Charlie, and she didn't want someone else announcing her arrival until she was ready.

Of course, she knew Charlie had been looking for her. Word had reached her several times via family members. Her brother had encouraged her for years to make contact. When she finally decided she would, he also tried to talk her out of it. "It's been five years. Send an email, a letter, a message via this private investigator bloke," he'd argued. "Don't show up on the poor bastard's doorstep!" But as always, Myra would do it her way and not take the advice of others.

As night descended, she drove towards to her hotel to contemplate how and when she would contact Charlie. She had been deep in thought when a kangaroo jumped out in front of her vehicle. Startled and swerving to miss, she corrected the car before pulling up at the side of the road to calm herself. She'd forgotten about the wildlife that could appear out of nowhere, especially at dusk. About to continue her journey, the police car startled her as it pulled up behind her.

"Shit!" she hissed.

The police officer got out of the car and walked towards her. The darkness obscured the man's identity, as she prayed it wasn't Sergeant Phil Cook.

Lowering her window in readiness, her heart raced and she felt short of breath.

"Hi," said the unfamiliar voice. "I saw the 'roo, you okay?"

Myra breathed a sigh of relief as the unknown policeman spoke to her.

"Yes, I'm fine. Just didn't see it. Gave me a bit of a fright. But I'm okay, thank you."

"Yeah, need to be careful around here. Especially at this time of night. Never know what's gonna come out of the bush: 'roo, wombat, possum."

"Thank you, officer. I'll pay a bit more attention," she said, smiling at the middle-aged man.

"You're not from around here, are you? Out for a drive, eh?"

"Something like that," she replied. "I should get going before it gets any darker. Wouldn't want to get myself lost out here."

The policeman laughed, agreeing with her before saying farewell.

That was a little too close, she thought as she drove back toward Yarra Junction.

¥

Back at the police station, the unknown officer returned and reported the events.

"Well?" asked Phil.

"I think it might be her," he replied. "She matched your description and, well, the photo you showed me. Hair's shorter and the colour's a bit different, but she definitely had a mole under her right ear."

"You didn't see her licence?"

"How could I? She hadn't done anything wrong. What was I going to say? You're going too fast. I just wanna get a look at you? I had no cause.

I was lucky a 'roo had jumped out in front of her and gave her enough of a fright to make her pull over."

"Yes, yes. Okay. Thanks. Now, to break the news to Charlie."

Phil Cook wanted to deliver the news in person but would prefer not in front of Ruby. It seemed Myra had left town again for the night, at least, so there was no urgent hurry. He would wait until he could get Charlie alone.

¥

Phil called Charlie and arranged to meet for lunch at the Powellie Pub. Charlie, curious, had been reluctant at first, but Phil had been insistent. There could only be one reason, thought Charlie.

The two sat making small talk as they drank a beer and waited for their meals. Charlie's frustration grew, wondering why Phil had invited him to lunch and did little more than talk about the weather.

"Cookie, as nice as it is to have lunch with you, is there a reason for this catch-up? I got the impression–"

"Yeah, sorry, Charlie. There is something. But it's a little delicate."

"I'm guessing it's to do with Myra?"

The police sergeant studied the man opposite, somewhat surprised at the comment.

"How did you know?"

"What else could be 'delicate'? In the past, whenever you've talked about Myra or the accident, you have a gloominess about you. A tone in your voice that says you'd rather be elsewhere. And you've got it now, even though we've been speaking about the cricket team!" Charlie laughed.

"Right. Yeah."

"So ... are you gonna tell me? Or do I have to guess?"

"Charlie, she was here in town yesterday."

Charlie stiffened before leaning back in the chair. He hadn't expected that.

"She was here? Did you speak to her?"

"No. But I'm pretty sure it was her."

"Pretty sure. But you're not 100 percent?"

"It was late yesterday afternoon. I was going into the general store when I noticed a woman in a car doing a U-turn. I thought she looked familiar, but she took off too quickly. I sent Mitchell to follow her and see if he could find out."

"Mitch wouldn't know her."

"Exactly. I didn't want to spook her if it was her. He's seen her picture and I described her to him ... anyway. A 'roo jumped out in front of her car. She had to swerve to miss it and got a fright, so pulled over. Mitchell took the opportunity to see if she was alright and checked her out. Her hair's shorter and changed colour, but there was definitely a mole under her right ear. I'm pretty sure it was her, Charlie."

Charlie no longer felt like eating. He'd waited for this moment for almost five years. Yet, he still didn't know if she'd returned or where she was staying. In many ways, he was no closer than before.

"So, what do I do now? Sit back and hope she shows up again?" Charlie said with exasperation.

"We got the registration plate. I've already searched on the number. It's a hire car from the city. She picked it up in Essendon two days ago and has hired it for a week. I've also called around to see if I can find out where she's staying. Her mother promises me she's not there and I haven't been able to get on to her brother yet."

"Do you believe Maureen?"

"Yeah, I do. She genuinely seemed surprised."

Charlie and Phil continued to talk, scarcely touching their food. With no choice but to wait, Charlie decided not to say anything to Ruby just yet. There may be nothing to tell her. Myra may have gone again, for all he knew.

Chapter Nineteen

Several days later, Ruby stood cleaning implements in the laundry when the phone rang. Ruby moved as quickly as she could to answer it before it went to message bank.

"Hello?" answered Ruby.

"Rusty, it's Cookie. How ya doin'?"

"I feel like a whale!" she said, laughing and rubbing the bulge. "And I'll be glad when this heat wave ends. God, it's impossible to get comfortable."

"Not long now. What ... about six weeks?"

"Four," she replied. "And it can't come quick enough. But I'm sure you didn't ring to ask about the pregnancy. What can I do for you?"

"Is Charlie there?"

"No. I expected him home an hour ago. Can I pass on a message?"

Phil hesitated before replying, "Yeah, if you like. We spoke the other day. Just let him know it's definite. Coming to town tomorrow. And ask him to call me."

Ruby remained silent, taking in the cryptic message.

"Ruby? You there?"

"Yeah, I'm here."

"Did Charlie fill you in on the latest?"

"Of course," she lied. "I just ... wasn't ..."

Phil breathed a sigh of relief. "Oh good."

"No. None of us were." Phil kept talking for what seemed like forever about how it would benefit Charlie, finally bringing this to a close, but Ruby heard little as her hand began to tremble.

As she replaced the receiver, Charlie walked in the front door. He smiled at her, kissed her on the head, and went to put his briefcase away.

"You okay?" he asked, eventually noticing the look on her face.

"Cookie rang."

"Oh? What'd he want? He asked.

"He said, 'it's definite' and 'give me a call'."

Charlie stared at Ruby perplexedly, not understanding the message.

"Did he say anything else? What is definite?"

"I don't know, Charlie. It seems once again you're keeping me out of the loop. What's '*the latest*'? Cookie thought you would have told me. Let me guess. Something to do with Myra?"

Charlie stopped what he was doing and turned to Ruby. He was now kicking himself for not having said anything to her before now. He understood how this looked to her, going behind her back again and, as she regularly accused him, of holding out hope that his previous life with Myra would return.

Speech failed to come. An apology would sound weak and hollow. There were no valid justifications. So he stayed silent.

"Were you going to tell me she was back?"

"Nobody had confirmed it."

"So, you thought you'd keep it to yourself."

"I didn't want you to find out like this. Cookie shouldn't—"

"Cookie thought you would have told me. I thought you would tell me something like this. But, no. Once again, we're back where we were, aren't we, Charlie? This whole secretive Myra thing that keeps coming between us."

"It's not like that."

"Then what's it like, Charlie? Why didn't you tell me? I'm about to have your baby," she said, voice raising in frustration. "I thought we were past this. Remember? Myra was gone and you weren't hiding things from me anymore!"

"I didn't want you to get upset when I didn't know if she was going to come and see me or not."

"Why else would she be back?! Charlie ... ah, forget it. I'm tired of Myra being in this relationship. I'm tired of trying to guess what you're going to do if she came back."

"I'm not going to do anything with her!"

"Aren't you? It constantly feels like you're having an affair with your absent wife. I feel like the other woman. You go, Charlie. You do whatever it is you need to do with her. I won't ask questions cos, obviously, it's a part of your life that I'm not a part of. When you're ready –if you're ready–your daughter and I will be waiting for you. But we won't wait forever, Charlie." Ruby turned and walked out of the room.

Charlie's head spun. What hold did Myra still have on him? Why did he keep it all to himself? The turmoil and confusion of five years came crashing back. He didn't know what he was feeling, what he thought, or what he was doing. How could he share that with Ruby?

Charlie went to find Ruby. As she prepared the evening meal in the kitchen, he placed his arms around her, saying, "I love you, Rubes."

Ruby didn't stop what she was doing and pushing his arms away as she kept working and challenged. "I'm sick of words, Charlie. Prove it."

¥

Laying in bed, with their backs to each other, neither Charlie nor Ruby slept. A great chasm seemed to have opened between them and Charlie didn't know how to breach it and Ruby didn't know if she wanted to. He tossed and turned with his thoughts and feelings, torn between the past and the present.

He rolled over, moving closer to spoon with Ruby. He placed his arm around her swelling belly and wept soundlessly at the confused mess he'd created. Silently, he scolded himself for allowing any of this to happen. He should have stuck with his original plan, find Myra, deal with her one way or another before moving on with someone who deserved better than what he was giving her. The baby kicked, pushing his hand. It served as a poignant reminder that such thoughts were pointless. What was he going to do to fix things?

Ruby rolled over to face him in the dark. A sniff from her told him she'd been weeping too.

"I'm sorry, Rubes," he breathed, holding her closer. "I'm so sorry."

"It's not all your fault," she responded. "You were honest from the beginning! You never lied to me about your confusion. I thought ... I thought I was strong enough for this."

"Well, the timing's not great, let's be honest," he said.

"It never is, Charlie," Ruby broke down. "Can we survive this?"

He hesitated before responding. "If life's taught me anything, it's taught me we have to."

"I meant together."

"Yeah, I know you did."

Hollow promises were not in him. He wouldn't anymore, he promised himself. He didn't have a clue about what the next day held, let alone the future, but didn't want to give her false hope.

Ruby rolled over again to face away from him. His words and embrace did not bring her comfort. She felt adrift on the sea with a broken mast. A distant storm was approaching and she was powerless against it. She cradled the baby she carried and silently wept.

The next morning, over breakfast, Ruby announced she thought it best for her to go away for a few days to give Charlie space to see Myra unencumbered. As Charlie protested, she proclaimed it may also be her last chance for a break before the baby arrived. She claimed she wasn't leaving permanently, but maybe a bit of space would be good for him to deal with the things he needed and she could rest at her sister's on the coast. While Charlie didn't like it, he agreed, finding comfort in the fact that her doctor and the hospital were only a few hours away in case of an early arrival.

The following day, Ruby left. Charlie watched as her car disappeared. He stood by the gate, staring into the distance with nothing but the sounds of the bush to keep him company. Toby barked on the other side of the block, pulling Charlie out of his thoughts. Toby barked often, but this was an unusual, persistent bark.

Charlie went to investigate. A six-foot snake lay basking in the warm summer sun.

"Toby!" Charlie called. "Here!"

Toby looked at his master and back at the snake and failed to obey.

"Toby!" yelled Charlie, approaching and yelling with a sterner voice. He stomped his feet hoping to scare the snake away. It was clear that the snake was a harmless python, not a venomous one. Nevertheless, he didn't want Toby to get into the habit of playing with snakes.

It reminded Charlie of how he and Ruby had spent a sleepless night together: watching over Toby after being bitten by a copperhead snake.

"Don't you go getting bitten now, mate. She's not here to save you this time," he sighed.

Charlie's mobile phone rang in his pocket. Hoping for a change of heart from Ruby, he quickly reached for the phone. The caller ID displayed "Col" and he felt his heart sink and considered not answering. He didn't want to have to explain his sister had gone away unexpectedly. He wasn't ready for all the questions. Answer it and get it over with, he told himself.

"Col. Hi mate," he said, answering with attempted enthusiasm.

"Charlie. How ya doin'? I just spoke to Rusty—or tried to. Phone kept cutting out. Sounded like she said she was going down the coast or something. Is that right?"

"Yeah, mate. She thought a break before the baby arrives could be good."

"You didn't go with her?"

"Obviously not, mate!"

"Sorry. Everything alright?"

"Yeah, yeah. You know, she's tired, I'm tired. A break will do her good. I've got a bit too much work on me plate ..."

"I hear ya! Look, if you're free, wanna grab a beer later? We could ring Simmo and ... maybe dinner?"

"You're breaking up a bit, mate, but yeah, dinner at the pub sounds good. You call Simmo. I gotta get to a meeting soon. I'll call you later."

"Okay, mate. Catch ya."

Charlie went back to the house with Toby in tow. The silence was overwhelming. He'd forgotten how quiet the house could be. He'd gotten used to hearing Ruby singing along to the radio. Now, it was strangely mute and he didn't like it. Charlie kicked himself. He didn't want to live in the in between world of sorrow. He needed to sort things out. He needed to find his wife and have the long overdue conversation with her. The next few days were crucial for him to address as much as he could and not waste them feeling sorry for himself.

¥

That evening, after a few phone calls to organise, Simmo, Col and Charlie went for a boy's night out. It had been a while since it was just 'the boys' and they each noted how great it felt. While they cherished their women, being free to talk sports, cars, and even their significant others was a welcome change.

Col, being Ruby's brother, meant Charlie felt he had to be a little careful. Col was a good bloke and understood some of the issues Charlie had, but he was in no hurry to announce Myra had returned and Ruby had gone away.

They met at Col and Lucy's new apartment near Chapel Street in a trendy part of Melbourne. While Col and Charlie mocked their friend and how he had changed, they relished an excuse to return to the city for a night. The outer suburbs were where they lived, but occasionally, the excitement of the city was a welcomed change.

Pete and Lucy's apartment had balcony views over the Yarra River and the historic suburb of Richmond. Pete swore you could see the Melbourne Cricket Ground from the balcony, but as Col and Charlie stood leaning as far over the rail as possible and straining, they could see nothing.

"You can almost hear the ball bounce on game day," Pete said, laughing.

Lucy rolled her eyes as Pete continued to exaggerate how close they were to the hallowed turf.

"Okay, I'm going," she announced. "I'll leave you lot to argue amongst yourselves. Just take everything he says with a grain of salt. I won't tell you about the number of times he complains about the traffic on game day or the noise on Saturday nights," she said before kissing Pete and leaving.

After a few more beers, sitting on the balcony and watching the sunset in the distance, they prepared to head up Chapel Street. The summer evening was warm and the sky was clear. With a ten-minute hike to The Jam Factory, they decided that was as good a place as any to begin the evening. Where they'd end up was anyone's guess, but for now, they would head out and see where their mood took them.

"Must cost you a bomb living here, mate," said Col as the three men entered the lift on the 6th floor.

"Not when you're a big shot city lawyer," Charlie said, digging Pete in the ribs.

"Certainly doesn't hurt, Chuckles," rebuffed Pete.

The men walked up the road, laughing and joking as they went. When they reached The Jam Factory, no one seemed able to decide on where to eat. Col didn't fancy seafood, while Pete could eat Asian food anytime with Lucy. Eventually, Charlie decided he fancied a steak. This, of course, began a new discussion that bordered on argument.

"We could go to the Prahran Hotel," suggested Charlie.

"Nah, that place isn't much chop," Pete said, laughing enthusiastically.

"Oh my goodness," said Charlie, rolling his eyes. "We're going to the 'dad jokes', are we?"

Col looked confused, not understanding the joke.

"Steak ... chop ... you know, a cut of meat ..."

"Gees, Simmo. That was terrible," Col said, once it had been explained. "Anyway, we all know the best *joint* is in the city."

Col and Pete continued to laugh at their attempted humour.

"If you two don't *cut* the puns, I'll give you the *chop*," said Charlie.

"Give us the chop ... ahahaha," laughed Pete.

"Don't laugh at him, Simmo. Charlie's got no *beef* with you."

"We could *steak* out that *joint* over there," said Pete.

"Have you finished?" asked Charlie.

"You don't like the puns. I thought they were *well done*!"

Charlie cracked. Unable to keep a straight face as his childhood friend continued to have fun with the steak jokes.

"Hey, what do you call a cow with a twitch?" asked Col. "Beef jerky!"

"What do you call a cow with two legs?" asked Pete. "A side of beef."

"What do you call a cow with one leg?" asked Col. "Steak." Col laughed at his joke while the other two looked at each other.

"That wasn't funny, Browny. In fact, that was crap. Gees, you might need to raise the *steaks* if that's the best you can do," said Pete.

"I'm starting to think tonight was a *mis-steak*?" said Charlie as the three men continued to walk up Chapel Street.

Before they knew it, they had walked for a good thirty minutes and were at High Street. They made their way to the nearby Prahran Hotel, eager for a drink. They would consider staying for a meal if it wasn't overly crowded and the food looked decent.

They walked in and looked around for a table. Seeing one in the far corner, Pete pointed, saying, "Why don't you *stake* a claim to that one while I get us some drinks?"

Charlie looked at him in disbelief as Pete snorted and walked towards the bar.

"Okay, okay. That was the last one. I promise," he said over his shoulder as Col and Charlie moved towards the table.

The hotel was packed with revellers enjoying the balmy summer evening. Many were eating meals and the men looked closely at the offerings as they walked through, sitting in one of the quirky, yet modern; round booths and waited for Pete to return.

Pete came back with three beers and menus. As they studied the menu, Col couldn't help himself. "Just one more," he began. "This place certainly charges–like a wounded *bull*."

While Col laughed, Pete and Charlie smiled but refused to reward their friend with a giggle, instead opting for a shake of the head and roll of their eyes.

The men then set the jokes aside as they drank their beers and decided what to eat. The conversation soon shifted to more serious topics anf Charlie admitted Ruby had gone to the coast. Questioning Ruby's sudden decision to leave for a few days, it seemed strange to Col, so close to her due date. It also surprised Pete to hear the news, as Charlie attempted to avoid answering their questions with a straight answer. Col and Pete were both suspicious and eventually challenged him head-on.

"I've known you a long time, mate. I know when you're hiding something. Now, spit it out. What's going on?" asked Pete.

"Col, this might be a little hard to hear, so please understand, I don't want to hurt Ruby. But the past has reared its head."

"Wha d'ya mean?" both Col and Pete asked simultaneously.

"Myra," he replied.

"Gees, Chuckles. And you've said nothing? What the fuck, mate?" said Pete, incredulously.

"There's not really been anything to say, Simmo."

"Obviously there's enough if Rusty's gone bush!" he said.

Col sat quietly listening as Charlie explained Myra was seen in the area, but as yet, had not contacted him. He was waiting for it to be confirmed before possibly upsetting Ruby. However, Myra hadn't contact him. He told of Phil Cook and Mitch had identified her and he was now trying to find where she was staying. He regretted that Ruby had to find out any of this from the police sergeant instead of himself.

"No shit, Sherlock!" said Pete.

"Easy, mate," said Col, trying to be understanding and supportive.

"Let me get this right. So, Rusty's left town so that you can sort things out with your misses?"

Charlie sat, nodding. "Pretty much."

"Is she coming back?" asked Pete.

"She said she would. In a couple of days—a week, maybe."

"Do you want her to come back, Charlie?" asked Col.

Charlie hesitated before being able to reply. "Mate, I can't move forward until I resolve the Myra thing."

"Nice sidestep, Charlie," said Pete.

"Gimme a break, Simmo. I've been living in hell for the best part of five years! I didn't want any of this to happen. Don't I deserve some answers?"

"Sure you do! But what about Ruby? What does she deserve? For Christ's sake, she's about to have your baby! And you let her walk off into the sunset, not knowing what you want with your ex-wife."

"She's not my ex-wife."

"And there we have it! Charlie, what are you thinking?" asked Pete. "This woman really did a job on you. Disappeared, was happy to let you possibly go to jail for an accident you didn't commit. And you still think of her as your wife."

"I don't 'think of her'; she is my wife!"

"Only by a technicality. In fact," he hesitated to do the maths, "she's been gone longer than you two were married. Rusty's been more of a wife to you in the last couple of years than Myra ever was! She's supported you with everything–including the shit of the accident. She allows you to have your fantasy chats with Issie G and even joins in with them. Myra would never do that. Fuck me, Myra probably doesn't even know where Issie's buried. Where was she when you needed her?"

"I know it sounds crazy."

"I thought you were a decent bloke, Charlie. I didn't expect you to do this to my sister."

"Do what? I haven't done anything!"

"That's the problem," said Pete.

"I just want answers," he stated finally.

"You be very careful, my friend. If you're not, you could lose the best thing to happen to you in years," said Pete.

Chapter Twenty

Charlie returned home the next day. The boys' night had been a disaster. After Charlie's revelations, no one was in the mood for a fun time. The words and sentiment of his trusted friend rang in his ears. As he opened the front door to the house, it smelled of Ruby, the furniture polish she insisted on using because of its smell. In the bedroom, he could smell her perfume. In the kitchen, he imagined he could smell their last meal together. Suddenly, he wondered what he was thinking, too. Simmo was right. Ruby was more of a supportive partner than Myra had ever been. It was not her fault, he thought, still making excuses for her. She was a city girl living in the country.

Stop it, he scolded himself.

Charlie gave himself a shake. He had work to do so headed to the study. He'd only just sat down when the phone rang. It was Cookie. Myra had reportedly been in touch. While she hadn't gone into everything with Phil, she'd explained enough. She asked Phil if he'd organise a meeting with Charlie, preferably in neutral territory and not at the block. She wanted to explain her side of events to him but was afraid of how Charlie would respond.

"She seems scared, Charlie," he explained.

"Well, that's ridiculous. Scared of what?"

"Scared you'll be angry."

"Don't I deserve to be angry, Cookie?"

"Yeah, but if you want answers, you're gonna have to control yourself."

"Gees, you make me sound like a monster. When have I ever been a threat to her?"

"Charlie, I'm just telling you what she said."

Silence fell on the line as Charlie took a deep breath. "Okay, when does she want to meet?"

"As soon as possible. She said she has to leave again in a week for a short time at least."

They soon arranged a date and time. The sooner the better for me, too, thought Charlie. They'd meet later in the week in Warburton. Far enough away from prying eyes and ears but close enough for both to reach effortlessly.

"She's changed, Charlie. She doesn't seem as self-assured as she once was. Go easy, eh?"

Charlie could feel the turmoil bubbling away as he got off the phone. He'd waited five years for his day. A part of him longed to see Myra again. How had she changed, he wondered. Parallel emotions of anger, disappointment, compassion and sadness were felt for her. He thought he knew her well enough and believed she had lived in hell for five years. He knew, without any doubt, that Myra had loved Isabella, but did she know where she was buried? His thoughts were interrupted by a second phone call.

"Charlie, it's Claire."

"Claire! Everything alright," he asked.

"Ruby's gone into labour."

Charlie jumped up from the desk. The baby wasn't due for weeks. Suddenly, concern filled his mind. Was it his fault? Had he caused her stress and the anxiety had set the labour in motion? Those thoughts had no place in the present moment. He had to get to Ruby.

"Where is she?"

"I'm taking her to the hospital. We're still a good hour away, but I think we've got time."

"We better have time!" Ruby called from the passenger seat. "I'm not having this kid on the side of the road. And you'd better fucking be there, Charlie!"

"Okay, maybe we don't have as much time as I thought," reported Claire.

"Is she okay?" Charlie asked, concerned.

"Yeah, this is normal. Just pray she's pissed at you and not in the second stage of labour, or we may have this baby on the side of the road."

Charlie got off the phone, grabbed his keys and headed for the hospital.

He arrived before Ruby and her sister, Claire, and paced the waiting room. Claire came in, rushing toward the triage nurse's desk while Ruby sat in the car, unable to walk. Charlie rushed outside to Ruby.

"I'll carry you," he offered.

"No! Claire's getting help. Charlie, I think something's wrong. It shouldn't hurt this much," she said before being gripped in pain.

Charlie's blood ran cold as he looked at the pale woman sitting in the front seat of her sister's car with a small pool of blood staining her trousers. He went into mechanical mode. Keep her calm.

"It's normal, sweetie. Hang in there. It'll all be over soon," he said, alarmed by what he saw.

A hospital attendant arrived with a nurse and a trolley to get Ruby to the delivery unit.

Charlie wiped the sweat from Ruby's brow and whispered reassurances as she was examined. The baby was in a breach position and it appeared the placenta was pulling away from the uterine wall, which explained the blood loss. It would be a difficult birth, but both the baby and Ruby were in no danger. They'd need extra monitoring and, if needed, an emergency C-section.

For the twenty-four hours, Ruby was in labour. Charlie stayed by her side, encouraging as much as he could. Finally, the baby was born. The trauma to the baby was apparent as it lay motionless and unresponsive. With suction to clear the airways and gentle massage, the baby began to breathe. The nursing staff wheeled the baby away to the ICU.

Ruby was exhausted and soon drifted to sleep. Charlie was reminded labour was taxing for both mother and baby. Suddenly, Charlie realised how tired he was, too. But he couldn't shake the feeling that the trauma of the birth wasn't over yet.

"Why don't you go and see your daughter," suggested the nurse. "Your wife will probably sleep for some time now."

"She's not–," Charlie stopped.

"Maybe you should go and get some sleep, too. It's been a long few days and Ms Brown is going to take a little while to recover. There was a significant tear, so she may have trouble with the most basic of things, like walking," the nurse advised.

"I'll stay if that's okay," he said.

Charlie dozed restlessly in the chair next to Ruby. At 5 a.m., he was woken when the nurse brought the baby in for a feed. The baby didn't seem interested and struggled to latch on correctly. After trying for half an hour, the nurses took the baby away again, saying they'd try again in a little while.

Alone, Charlie and Ruby sat in silence for some time. Words seemed to fail in Charlie's throat.

"How are you?" Ruby finally asked.

"Huh," Charlie huffed. "I should be asking you that."

"I'm as well as can be expected."

"Are you in much pain?"

"Not too much. More tired than anything."

Charlie nodded.

"Have you seen her?" Ruby asked.

Charlie stared intently at Ruby. "She was just in here. Yeah, I saw her."

"Not our daughter." The harsh tone evident.

"We need to decide on the name. I'm happy with Jasmine if that's what you like."

"Don't avoid the question, Charlie. You know who I'm talking about."

"No," he said. "We were meant to meet today, but I'm going to cancel it. I don't think I'm up to it."

"So you've spoken to her, then?"

"No, Cookie did. We made arrangements through him."

"Rose."

"Sorry?"

"I'd like to call her Rose."

"Okay. I'm happy for you to decide."

Ruby turned her head away as a tear fell. "She's your daughter too, Charlie. It should be a joint decision, shouldn't it?" Ruby rolled over and tried to sleep again, leaving Charlie once again confused. It didn't seem to matter what he said or did, he was in the wrong.

¥

Charlie had just made it home in the late afternoon when Billy knocked and let himself in.

"Wasn't sure if you'd be here," he said, seeing Charlie lazing in a big armchair with the afternoon sun falling on him.

"Yeah, I'm here."

"Congratulations! You decided on a name for me niece?"

"No," said Charlie, simply.

Billy had heard from others that Myra was back and Ruby had gone just before the baby was born. While he hadn't spoken with Charlie, he knew his brother would be struggling. Charlie had always been a sensitive soul and, while someone may hurt him, he always found a way to empathise with them. There's always a reason, he'd say.

Billy watched his brother as he came into the room and sat. He saw no signs of excitement about his new daughter's birth. If anything, he didn't seem present.

Charlie stood. He walked with head down and shoulders stooped, offering a drink to Billy. He was a man carrying the weight of the world. They move into the kitchen and Charlie instinctively put the kettle on for a cuppa.

"Cup of tea time, is it?" Billy asked with a smile.

"Sorry, mate."

"Thought you'd want to wet the baby's head, but not with a cuppa."

Charlie looked up abruptly. He looked at the clock, then back at his brother.

"Beer o'clock, you reckon?"

"Only if you want one."

"Yeah ... yeah, why not?" Charlie said, more to please his brother than out of desire. The flat tone not missed by Billy.

"You okay, Charlie?" Billy asked.

"Yeah, sorry, mate. Just got a few things on my mind."

"Anything you want to talk about?"

"Nah. Bit tired after the long labour, you know."

Billy knew it went beyond the birth, but also knew if he wasn't careful, Charlie would shut down completely and not talk. Instead, he started talking of the superficial: the cricket results, the heat wave, and the effects of the drought on local farmers. "Probably don't need to tell you about their problems," Billy said. "You're no doubt helping them with water management."

"We're trying a few new techniques out at Robson's property and Jimmy's vineyard. Stuff they're doing in The States. Not convinced it's gonna be so successful here, but we'll see."

The small talk continued as they moved to the back deck and sat in silence. Billy listened to the babbling creek as Charlie offered to get refills.

“Cheers,” he said, handing a beer to Billy.

"I've heard the rumours, Charlie," said Billy, finally addressing the elephant in the room.

"Thought you would have," replied Charlie. "Surprised it's taken you an hour to bring it up."

"What are you going to do?"

"I don't really want to talk about it."

"So, head-in-the-sand Charlie, is it? "

Charlie didn't reply.

"Come on, you prick. It's me! Billy! Your brother. I know all your secrets. Don't you think they're safe with me?" he said, drawing the man out of his trance. "For instance, I recall you raiding the apple tree and discarding the evidence by the river when Dad thought the birds had eaten all the good ones. You were only twelve then. And I never told Dad."

Charlie turned to face his brother with a look of surprise.

"And I know it was you who put all that crap in Milly Sander's bag at school cos you thought she was an alien or something." Billy laughed.

"Shit, you were only a little kid then. How did you know about that?"

"I idolised my big brother," he said. "I watched everything you did. Even replicated some of your tricks."

Charlie laughed, "Is that why you put a bunch of sticks in Mum's shopping basket a couple of times?"

"Yeah, I didn't like her going shopping without me."

"I got the blame for that!"

"Yeah, I know. That's why I stopped. Didn't mean to get you in trouble."

"Why didn't you say anything?"

"You would have killed me! And then Mum and Dad would have given me the same punishment they gave you. I wasn't that stupid."

The pair chuckled as they shared childhood memories.

The evening wore on. The sun set and the night grew cooler. Still the conversation was stunted as they continued to sit on the deck.

"Nine o'clock. Wait for it," Charlie said.

They sat in silence and listened as the night chorus of the kookaburras began ten minutes later. The song echoed around The Valley as Mother Nature turned in for the night.

"You can almost set your watch by them," said Billy.

"Yep. Remember we used to say to Mum, 'It's not bedtime yet; the kookas haven't said goodnight'?

"And most times, she'd agree with us," said Billy, standing. "'nother beer?"

"I'll get 'em," replied Charlie taking the empty can from Billy.

With Toby following close behind, Charlie took the empties to the recycle bin before returning to the fridge. Toby crept along beside his master as Charlie got two more beers and a dog treat. Toby munched on the snack while Charlie watched him, deep in thought for a moment, before returning to the back deck.

"I don't know what to think, mate," Charlie said, walking outside and passing a beer to Billy. Billy said nothing.

"What am I supposed to do? I mean, do I approach her? Or wait for her to approach me? Do I let her give me an explanation? Or not?"

"You've been wanting this moment for years. Of course, you ask her to explain."

"And then what? 'Thanks for coming, and giving me an explanation, Myra. Have a good life. Oh, by the way, I have a new family."

"I don't know what she's going to do, mate, but I know what you'll do. She'll start talking and you'll start to feel sorry for her."

"Maybe she has a plausible explanation!"

"So you already feel sorry for her? Charlie, the big-hearted saviour of the world. It's not that simple anymore, Charlie."

"Why?"

"Because of Rusty and Bubs," Billy said. "It's one or the other and I think that's what's tearing you apart. You don't wanna let anyone down and you know you're going to have to. The real question for you, in my opinion, is who do you love more? Rusty or Myra."

Standing by the rail looking out into the dark bush surrounding the block, Charlie turned to look at Billy.

"Do you think I still love Myra? After all she's done to me?"

"If you didn't, this wouldn't be so hard for you. It'd be a case of see her, get the answers you want, serve her with divorce papers, and say goodbye."

"Fuck! You might be right." Charlie paused. "I didn't have time to really stop loving her. She just disappeared."

"Don't romanticise it though, mate."

"What do you mean?"

"The woman you fell in love with all those years ago isn't the woman that disappeared, not wanting to be found and leaving you to bury your daughter alone. You don't know this woman that's waiting for you. And, if you're not careful, you may lose a real woman that adores you and has stood by you while you've treated her like crap—no, I won't take it back. You have, and you know it."

"So what the fuck do I do?" Charlie yelled at his brother. "Cookie's arranged for me to see her!"

"Who cares? She's kept you waiting for years. Let her wait a few days," Billy said, incredulously.

"Go bush. Ruby's going to be in hospital for a few more days. Go bush, clear your head. I'll talk to Ruby and explain."

"Explain what? That I may still be in love with my wife?"

"Well, I might be a little more tactful than that! But if I know Ruby, she'll be understanding and happy to let you go. It’s what she wants! For you to once and for all deal with your feelings for Myra."

Chapter Twenty One

Charlie left early the next day. With Toby in the truck, they headed north. With no actual destination in mind, Charlie drove toward the Murray River and the state border. For several hours, he drove without wanting to get on the Hume Highway. He passed Yea and Euroa and knew he would soon need to decide on a destination. How ironic, he thought.

Charlie saw a sign for Shepparton and, turning to Toby, said, "How about morning tea in Shep, Tobes? Then we can decide where to from there."

Sleeping on the back seat, Toby opened his eyes at the mention of his name but wasn't interested enough to lift his head. Choosing, instead, to go back to sleep.

Charlie stopped at a service station on the other side of the city where Toby could have a run around in the adjoining field. Nearing midday, the day was already sweltering. Despite a clear sky above, Charlie saw the dark clouds of a summer storm looming ahead.

By early afternoon, he'd reached Barmah Lake and was surprised to see how many people were there. Summer was at its peak and it was the school holidays, so it shouldn't have been surprising. However, finding a place relatively secluded to set up the tent and equipment didn't take too long.

For two days, Charlie and Toby swam, walked, slept and did anything and everything to occupy their time. Charlie thought about Myra and Ruby but couldn't quite grasp his feelings. The baby crossed his mind and he wondered if Ruby had already named her. He still didn't feel like the father of this little creature he'd helped bring into this world. He wanted to be a good father to her, but he felt no love or connection.

This added to the guilt Charlie was feeling.

Charlie received a message from Billy saying he'd spoken with Ruby and she was glad he'd gone away for a few days. She hoped it would be beneficial.

Before he knew it, it was time to pack up and leave the sanctuary behind. He couldn't hide away forever and needed to return to the real world.

When he arrived home later that day, he was surprised to find Ruby sitting in a lounge chair watching the television with the baby nestled in her arms.

"What are you doing here?" he asked. "I wasn't expecting to pick you up until tomorrow. You should have called. I would have come back."

"Charlie, it's okay!" reassured Ruby. "You needed some time to clear your head and I needed some things, so came home. Col picked us up."

"How long have you been here?"

"A few hours. You just missed Col, actually. He was planning on staying, but I convinced him I'd be fine on my own."

Charlie moved closer and kissed Ruby before saying, "It's good to see you."

They smiled at each other awkwardly as Charlie moved towards the kitchen.

"You want a cuppa?"

"Yes, thanks," replied Ruby.

"How's Bub doin'?" he asked.

"She's okay. Seems to be getting the hang of this feeding thing, which is good. Not sure I am, though. It's pretty painful."

Charlie smiled, "Yeah, it'll pass." His mind was taken back to a similar conversation with Myra years earlier. "Have you decided on a name?"

Ruby sighed. "I we could do it together."

"Yes, of course!" said Charlie, regretting the sound of the question. "I just thought ... Fuck, Rubes, I don't know what I thought. Of course, I want to name her with you."

"You haven't even touched her since you came in."

"Here, give her to me. Let me look at her. Maybe I can see what she looks like."

Charlie took the sleeping child from Ruby's arms and could feel the torment inside himself. A part of him felt repulsed, as though he was being unfaithful to Isabella, which he knew was ridiculous. He had to bond with this little person as he had with his dead daughter, but it couldn't be forced.

The baby squirmed in his arms before settling again as Charlie gently rocked and soothed her. He examined her face and features for something that may look familiar. He saw nothing.

"You still keen on Rose?" he asked.

"Yeah? Maybe. But ... maybe not? I don't know. She just doesn't look like a Rose or a Jasmine."

"Margaret. Or Sinead."

Ruby laughed. "I don't think so. I was thinking something a little more Australian and a little more modern."

"Then Gertrude's out, I suppose, after my great-grandmother."

"Out! Definitely, out!"

"Hmm." Charlie examined his daughter.

"Something Australian. Matilda?"

"No."

"Kylie."

"Stop it! I'm not naming my daughter after your celebrity crush!"

Charlie was concentrating on the baby girl's face when she opened her eyes and stared up at him. At first, it seemed disconcerting, but he held her gaze until she again closed her eyes.

"Georgia Zoe," he said.

"Georgia Zoe?" Ruby repeated. "Hmm ... Georgie Porgie. No, can't have that. But maybe Zoe Georgia?"

"Zoe Georgia," Charlie said to the bundle in his arms that again opened her eyes. "I think she likes it," he said.

"Zoe," repeated Ruby. "I think I like it."

Charlie passed the baby back to her mother, who continued to look at her, repeating the name. "Zoe. Zoe, clean your room! Zoe, can you feed the dog? I like it!" she said, looking at Charlie.

"Then Zoe it is."

Charlie crouched beside Ruby and placed an arm around her shoulder. "You did good, you know?"

"Couldn't have done it without you," she said, kissing Charlie on the cheek. "I've missed you."

"Yeah," replied Charlie. "Sorry I haven't been a bit more on board. Still gotta face the demon," he said.

Ruby frowned. "When will that be?" Ruby asked stiffly.

"I'm hoping tomorrow," he said. "Thought I'd give Cookie a call and see if he can set something up. I don't have her number and don't want it," he added quickly. "Do everything through Cookie."

Charlie had walked away from Ruby and was busying himself in the kitchen making tea. While his words said one thing, Ruby thought his body language was saying something else. She wasn't entirely clear about what.

Chapter Twenty Two

The meeting with Myra was set for the following morning. Myra only had a short time as she'd said she needed to leave for an appointment elsewhere but would return in a week. Charlie needed to figure out what to make of this. Why was she returning in a week? He put it out of his mind. For now, he just wanted to get this meeting over and done with once and for all.

He rose early and went over the coming conversation a dozen times in his head. Each scenario a little different: he hears her out with no emotion; he releases five years of anger; finds the middle ground between the two; she begs him for forgiveness and asks him to take her back; she produces divorce papers and says that is the only reason she's come back. The bottom line, he had no idea how to prepare for the meeting.

Ruby found him sitting on the deck with his morning coffee, watching Toby playing at the edge of the river with, most likely, a yabbie or small fish. Zoe was still sleeping as Ruby sat gingerly beside Charlie. She placed a hand on his arm and squeezed.

"You okay?" she asked lovingly.

"I'll be glad when this is over," he replied.

"You and me both," she whispered more to herself.

¥

Phil Cook had arranged for Charlie to meet with Myra at 9:30. The day was warm but overcast. In the car, Charlie listened to the radio as broadcasters debated the weather: will it rain, won't it? Charlie listened but had little interest.

He arrived at the small, secluded café in Warburton a short time later. Charlie heaved a deep sigh before heading toward the café. The day he'd been waiting for had arrived. Butterflies and nervous energy ran rampant through his body.

Charlie entered the café and looked around. An older couple sat by the window enjoying scones with cream; another two women sat at a table, deep in a conversation he couldn't quite hear. But Myra wasn't there. He moved to a booth and sat down. From here, he could see the door and when she'd arrive.

The waitress came with a menu and he said he'd wait as he was meeting someone. As she walked away, Charlie could see Phil Cook talking with someone through the café window. He was surprised until he realised Phil spoke with Myra. She was here. The vague doubt that she may change her mind and not show up left. Charlie squirmed and repositioned himself in his seat as he saw the woman who looked familiar yet different opened the door to the café.

She hesitantly looked around before spotting Charlie at the booth. The two strangers faced each other without smiling or exchanging affection. Charlie stood and waited for her to reach the table. They then stood looking at each other for an eternity before Charlie ushered Myra into the booth.

"I wasn't sure you'd come," Myra said.

"Why? I've been looking for you for five years," he replied.

"Ouch!"

"Sorry, just seemed ... Sorry, let's start again."

Myra nodded.

"I'm sorry, Charlie. I'm ... not sure ..."

"Yeah, I know. Me too."

"You've probably got lots of questions."

"Yeah, one or two," he said, attempting to smile.

"Unfortunately, I don't have long. I need to catch a plane this afternoon. But I wanted to see you; start something. I'll be back next week. If you want, we can catch up again then and talk more."

"What happened, Myra?" Charlie said, abandoning the unimportant parts of the conversation. "You just vanished. And then, when you were found, you didn't want me. Why?"

"Charlie, I know this has been hard for you—"

"I don't think you do!"

"But it's been hard for me, too."

Charlie raised his eyebrows, holding back the words that he wanted to say. Let her talk, he kept telling himself. Let her say what she needs to say first.

Myra seemed to talk without actually saying anything. Charlie listened as she told of her move to London, Switzerland, and China. All the while, she was running from the past as fast as she could because of what she'd done. Eventually, she realised she wouldn't have peace until she stopped running and faced up to Charlie.

"And that's why you're here," Charlie stated. "Nothing to do with finding out where your daughter's buried or see how I'm doing. We never came into the equation; you just needed to clear your conscience." Charlie could feel the bile rising as he sat before the woman he once loved with all his heart.

The waitress returned to take their orders but neither seemed to notice. Sensing the tension, she gathered the menu and walked away.

"I have no excuses good enough to pardon what I did, Charlie. I know that. I know that I've put you through hell."

"I've been in a limbo world for five years, Myra!" Charlie exclaimed a little louder than he intended.

The waitress appeared with glasses of water and gave Charlie a questioning look. "Everything okay, here?" she asked Myra. Myra nodded and smiled as the waitress again retreated.

"Just tell me what happened that day you left," he asked more calmly.

Myra gathered her thoughts and sighed. "It had been the day after the storm, remember? As you always seemed to do, you'd gone off to help clean up around the place and I returned home with the baby."

"Isabella, in case you've forgotten her name," said Charlie cruelly.

"I know her fucking name, Charlie. I can recount every dimple on her body, the exact length of her fingernails, and not a day goes by when I don't ache for her!"

Charlie looked at Myra and saw, for the first time, the actual pain she was carrying. In a few quick minutes, she'd turned from an insecure woman to one of purpose.

"I know where she is buried," she continued. "When I recovered, I found out. The toys around her grave are incredible!" she said, looking at Charlie. "Yes, I've visited her. Almost every day since I've been back."

"What were you recovering from?" Charlie asked.

"Huh," chuckled Myra, "the list is quite long! We probably don't have time to go into it right now."

"What do you want from me, Myra? If you want to say your piece, then now's the time. If it's making any sort of announcement, the floor is yours. Tell me what you need to and go catch your plane," Charlie said despondently.

"I don't want just to make my peace, Charlie. Like you, I've been stuck in limbo and the only way we can get out of that is together."

Charlie looked at the woman opposite but said nothing.

"I thought," she began, "I would quickly give you the story from my side. Some of it you're not going to like. But I ask you to listen, anyway. Then, next week, when you've had a chance to digest what I've said, you can tell me what life has been like for you. Whether or not I like it, I've hurt you and I have to hear, feel, and deal with what I've done."

"And then? What? We go our separate ways and live happily ever after?"

"That's as far as I'd got. Then it's up to you."

They sat in silence for a minute, looking at each other.

"Not here," Charlie said. "This isn't a conversation for a café. You got time to go up the mountain? Not far, just up the road a bit."

Myra nodded.

They went outside to see Phil Cook waiting for Myra. He said he had a few errands to run, so if Myra wanted a lift back to Gilderoy, he'd pick her up in an hour outside the café.

Charlie and Myra got in Charlie's truck and set off for Mt. Donna Buang. On the summit, a cooler breeze blew as they got out at the deserted picnic ground. The pair sat at a table in the sun.

"I was angry with you that day, Charlie. Since Issie was born, you seemed never to be there when I needed you most. I didn't know it then, but I suffered post-natal depression. I felt like all I did was feed, change and hold her. I never had my hands free for longer than half an hour. I had no time to myself, and my husband seemed nowhere in sight. I was lonely, Charlie."

"Why didn't you say something?"

"Because I felt like a failure. I didn't know what I was feeling or why I was feeling it, so how could I express that? I'd gone from being a career businesswoman, always meeting and speaking with people, to being isolated and alone with this little person that, at the time, I didn't think liked me very much."

"She adored you! How could you think that?"

"I know that now. But at the time, I didn't understand it was all linked to hormones and depression."

"I'm sorry you felt that, Myra."

"Anyway, I returned home while you went off with Simmo, Billy, or whoever. Issie cried all the way home and I thought I would go mad. I fed her, changed her, and put her down for a nap, but she was really unsettled. I was becoming more and more agitated, so left her in her crib and went to check the chickens' coop for eggs. When I got to there, I noticed a hole in the wire. I started trying to fix it, but it took longer than expected.

"After a while, I thought I'd better check on the baby, so started heading back to the house. I heard a door slam and wondered if you were home. At the back door, I heard a noise that wasn't Issie. I looked in on the baby and she seemed to have settled, so wandered around the house to work out what the noise had been. There was nothing there, so I went back out to the chicken coop with the baby monitor.

"It wasn't long and I heard the baby crying again and instantly, I was on edge. I left her to grizzle for a bit and continued with the retched coop. Is she never going to give me any peace? I kept thinking. I nearly had the coop fixed, but the baby was getting louder. I remember thinking, 'Just two more minutes, baby. Just let me finish!' But I was so agitated by this stage, the more I pulled on the chicken coop, the bigger the hole seemed to become. It completely transfixed me, so much so that I left Issie, who by this stage was... screaming!

"Then, I heard the car. I was a little dazed or something cos I remember looking up and couldn't quite understand what was happening. Who was in the car? And why were they driving at the house? Next thing I knew, there was a ball of fire where the house stood. I was laying on the ground. I didn't know if I'd been unconscious or what happened. I was numb for a minute before heading towards the house. I can't remember much other than one minute I was at the chicken coop, the next, my arm was on fire. There was a second explosion and I remember thinking, 'There's nothing I can do, so I might as well leave'."

Myra had a glassy, distant look in her eyes as if seeing it play out before her again. Charlie sat waiting for more, but Myra had stopped talking.

Eventually, he asked, "Where did you go?"

"I walked through the bush. I don't know how long, but I remember sleeping in the open air. I had an infected arm, and I was sick when someone found me in pretty bad shape."

"What did you do?"

"The people that found me were foreigners hiking and camping in the bush. Their English wasn't great, but I convinced them to take me to Warbie and my GP."

"Susan? She never said..."

"No, doctor-patient confidentiality. I asked her not to say anything. She cleaned me up and I decided to disappear."

"Just like that."

"Not 'just like that', Charlie. I was in hell! My daughter was dead because of me, because I had decided fixing the chicken coop was more important than her. I was delirious! I lied to Susan about my arm. How could I face you and tell you that? I was ashamed enough at not being able to cope as a mother. I couldn't face you and tell you I'd killed her!"

Myra's voice wavered as she said, "She was your Issie G. She was your world. I felt nothing but broken since she'd been born. I didn't need to hear you reject me, as I was sure you would. You were better off without me around."

Charlie was speechless. What on earth could he say to that? He felt torn again between compassion and anger for his wife. He wanted to understand and forgive. But could he? He didn't know.

"Surely, you got the message when the police initially found you. I wanted to see you, Myra. I wanted to understand. I wanted to put this behind me. Behind us! But you deserted me."

"I know, and I will be eternally sorry for that, Charlie. I made a mistake. Huh, it would seem I made quite a few mistakes. But it wasn't all my fault. I was mentally unstable. I lost myself when Isabella was born and you weren't around to save me. I went from one poor decision to another, racked with pain and guilt. Finally, a few months back, I had two choices: come back and face what I'd done or ... end my life. I couldn't live the way I was any longer."

Charlie listened to the words struggling to comprehend, not knowing how to respond. "Have you been getting help?" he asked.

"Yeah, I began seeing a psychiatrist twelve months ago. It's taken this long to have the strength to come back. But I'm here, Charlie. And I want to work through this, for both our sakes, if you give me a chance."

Charlie raised himself from where he had been sitting and walked towards Myra. As he approached, she looked at him, full of anxiety and apprehension. The chasm between them shrank as Charlie sat beside his wife and put his arms around her, pulling her close. This woman, no matter what she'd done or why she'd done it, was the only other living person on the face of the earth who knew what he'd gone through. He had a lot of work to do before he could forgive and forget. But she was the key to his healing.

Charlie and Myra sat in the picnic ground of the national park, clinging to each other as two people clinging to a life raft, afraid of letting go in case they drowned. They had barely kept themselves above water for so long time, being rescued was a much-needed break.

Charlie held Myra's tear-stained face in his hands as he kissed her. Time stood still for the grieving pair that could finally grasp the other, a lifeline to get out of the mire.

"Oh, Myra," Charlie said, "I'm sorry I wasn't there."

Again, they held each other with no more words. What else was there to say? Charlie released the grip he had on her before standing and pacing. He sat again before saying, "I don't know where we go from here. Maybe we need counselling or something, but we'll work it out, okay?"

Myra nodded back at Charlie silently.

"What time do you need to go?" he asked.

"About now," she replied with a sad smile. "But I'll be back."

Charlie nodded and thought of Ruby. What was he going to tell her?

As if reading his thoughts, Myra said, "I know you've moved on, Charlie. And I believe congratulations is in order."

Charlie looked at Myra with a pained stare.

"I don't want to cause more anguish for you or anyone else, Charlie. I will not take you away from your girl. I'll stay as long as needed to sort ourselves out and then go. I won't hold you back anymore."

"Promise you'll call as soon as you get back next week," he said.

Myra promised as they prepared to return to town and say good-bye.

Chapter Twenty Three

Charlie returned home to Ruby and baby Zoe, feeling conflicted. A strange sense of relief engulfed him after meeting Myra and hearing what she had to say. But he was returning home to another woman and child.

The anguish on his face evident to Ruby as she sat, listening as Charlie retold what Myra had said.

"And you believe her?" Ruby asked.

"Why shouldn't I?" Charlie replied a little defensively.

"Just checking," Ruby said.

"Look, I know this is hard for you, but we both wanted no more secrets. As you've told me, you are a part of my life now, so I'm trying to include you. If it's too much, then just say and I won't say any more."

"No secrets, Charlie."

Charlie sat, nodding.

"Are you going to see her again?"

"Yes," replied Charlie, calmly. "Next week, when she returns."

"Don't take this the wrong way, but can I ask why?"

"It's hard to explain."

"Try," she requested with a hard tone.

Charlie thought about the logical explanation before replying. "For five years, both of us have been living without resolution. I'm not sure you ever fully get over what we've been through. The hardest part for me was knowing she was out there somewhere and could possibly give me some answers. Why did she run away? Why wouldn't she see me? What was she doing? She didn't want to see me but didn't want a divorce either. So, what did she want? And from what Myra told me this morning, she's been living with guilt and shame over what she did. The only way forward for either of us is to talk. No one else will ever understand what we've been through. Losing a child, a life ..."

Ruby remained silent for a while, attempting to be both supportive and understanding. However, she sensed Charlie was holding something back. He almost seemed excited to be seeing Myra again next week. Ruby felt she was again being pushed out but would not go down without a fight.

"Can I meet her?" she asked.

Charlie looked surprised. He hadn't thought of the two women in his life having contact and didn't know what to say.

"Can I meet her, Charlie?"

"Why?"

"Charlie, you keep thinking this thing is yours and yours alone. Sorry, yours and Myra's alone. You allowed me into your life. You said it wouldn't be easy and I accepted that. This is far from easy for me but doesn't change the fact that I am now a part of this as well. Unless there is something you want to hide."

"No! No, of course not. Myra is the past. You and Zoe are my future. I just need to fix the transition from one to another with closure."

"Then let me help. Don't shut me out now, Charlie."

"You're right—as usual. Maybe—" Charlie looked at Ruby. "Maybe for the anniversary this year, we could invite Myra for dinner and she could join us in Issie's Garden."

Ruby nodded, relieved yet uncomfortable that Charlie had suggested inviting Myra to their anniversary ritual.

¥

Myra returned a week later, as promised, and soon after settling into her hotel called Charlie to arrange a meet up. At first, they were a little awkward around each other. While they each looked and sounded similar to the person they'd known, neither was the same person.

Charlie asked how long Myra would be in The Valley. "Not sure. Long enough to make amends with you?" she replied, leaving the answer open to interpretation.

"The anniversary is next week," Charlie said.

"I know. On the twenty-third."

"This might sound a little strange but each year I... ah, spend some time with Issie."

Myra raised her eyebrows in surprise.

"Oh? And what exactly does that mean?"

"Well, we usually go to the cemetery and lay flowers and, when no one is looking, tell her I'll meet her in the garden."

Myra frowned, not understanding. "What garden? And who is 'we'?"

"It used to be me and the boys. The first few years, we went out the night before the anniversary, get ridiculously drunk and sleep the next day away. Then, it turned to a barbeque at the block. We'd get ridiculously drunk and–"

"Sleep the next day away," Myra finished for him.

They both smiled and laughed.

"But I'd always make sure I went to the cemetery, tell her she was loved and missed."

"And what garden did you 'meet' her in?"

"The one I made for her at the block. Last year, I didn't want to drink the day away, so the two of us just had a few drinks in the garden and talked to Issie, you know."

"Ah! Your new lady," said Myra, looking suddenly uncomfortable. "She must be very understanding, indulging in your slightly morbid rituals. Not to mention letting you meet with your wife like this."

"She is. She's a good woman," replied Charlie reflectively. "In fact, I suggested inviting you for dinner and joining me in the garden to talk to Issie and she agreed. She'd ... we'd like you to come over."

"I'd like that, Charlie, but you don't think it will be awkward?"

"I guess that's up to us."

Their morning together went quickly. They caught up on the other's life, The Valley gossip and grew more comfortable around each other.

¥

The day of the anniversary came and Myra arrived at the block. Everyone acted politely but felt awkward. Both women felt like intruders on the other's turf, vying for one man's attention. While Charlie tried to make Myra feel welcome, he didn't want to upset Ruby. Eventually, Ruby sensed the right thing to do would be to suggest Charlie and Myra visit the cemetery while she prepared dinner for the three of them.

Charlie and Myra were gone much longer than Ruby had expected and couldn't help but feel slightly anxious. "Don't do this to yourself," she said as Toby looked quizzically at her. "They'll be here soon enough." Turning to the sleeping baby Zoe, she said, "Daddy's not going to be a dick, is he, Sweetheart? Daddy's gonna come back to us. I know it feels like he's been more absent than here for six months, but we have to be patient. And Daddy better sort his shit out soon, darling or Mummy's gonna take you away. If he wants her back–"

The sound of car doors closing interrupted her monologue. Ruby glanced in the mirror to ensure she looked as good as any woman who had only recently given birth. She busied herself as she waited for the front door to open. Ruby moved to the window to see what they were doing, only to see them entering Issie's Garden. She clutched her arms to her chest. He'd gone to the garden without her. She studied the woman standing, looking elegant, holding Charlie's hand. All of a sudden, Ruby felt like a country bumpkin intruding on someone else's land. She swallowed the tears she felt welling and put on a brave face. She would join them in the garden.

As Ruby approached, Charlie dropped Myra's hand and stepped away from her. However, Myra swiftly lessened the distance again.

"I thought I heard you arrive," Ruby said as pleasantly as she could muster.

"Sorry, Myra was keen to come to the garden," replied Charlie before officially introducing the women. "Where's Zoe?"

"Asleep."

"Zoe, is your daughter?" Myra said to Ruby.

"Our daughter, yes."

"Oh, how lovely for you." Myra continued to only address Ruby when speaking of the baby. "Let's hope nothing happens to her. I don't think Charlie has room for another memorial garden on the block. This one is so big."

The insensitive remark surprised Ruby, but she didn't know what to make of it. Whether Charlie heard it or not, she wasn't sure. He certainly didn't give any outward sign of it.

Silence fell on the group as they stood uncomfortably together.

"Should I leave you two?" asked Ruby, looking to Charlie for direction.

"Okay–" said Myra.

"No–" said Charlie simultaneously.

Just then, the cry of the baby made the decision a lot easier. As Ruby walked away, Charlie came after her.

"Rubes," he called.

"It's okay, Charlie. You go and be with Myra. I feel a little out of place and ... don't want to make things any more awkward than they already are."

“Don’t be like that, Ruby.”

“Charlie! Is this a poisonous plant you’ve put in a child’s garden?” called Myra.

Charlie turned to look at Myra without replying. When he turned back to Ruby, she had walked away. Charlie stood looking in both directions. Ruby plodded back to the house to tend to their child while Myra scrutinised the plants in the garden. Charlie surmised this hadn’t been such a great idea.

“Gimme a minute, My. I just need to check on Ruby,” he yelled over his shoulder, hurrying to the house.

Charlie entered the living room to see Ruby crying. He came to her but couldn’t bring himself to touch her. He felt no matter what he did, he would be betraying someone.

“Are you alright?” he asked.

“Yes, sorry. Just the hormones... you know,” Ruby replied without looking at him.

Charlie knew Ruby had been very teary since the birth of the baby, but how much was hormones and how much was him, he couldn’t decide. He could see Myra in the garden, sitting serenely, waiting for his return.

“Please, come out and bring Zoe when you’re finished feeding.”

“Oh, I think it best I stay here. You go back to Myra,” she said with a forced smile. "You wanted closure, remember?”

Charlie looked again towards Myra before saying, “I won’t be long.”

“I think you will be,” Ruby muttered under her breath sarcastically.

Charlie returned to Myra. They sat on the bench seat, side by side, to talk to their deceased daughter. They recalled the few memories they had of their baby girl. Charlie spoke of all the imaginings he’d had of Issie and what she’d be doing: helping in the herb garden, sitting on the ride-on lawnmower with him, getting ready to start school.

Myra stood up, a pained look on her face as she looked around.

"What is it?" Charlie asked.

"I'm just trying to remember," she said, looking around. "This, this is where the house used to stand, isn't it?" she said.

Charlie stood up. "Yes."

"And this would have been about where her ..." Myra looked at Charlie with pain-filled eyes. "Her bedroom was and where she died," she whispered as the tears began.

Charlie embraced Myra, clasping her tightly as she sobbed uncontrollably for the first time since the incident.

"It's okay, Myra. I'm here."

"I just left–"

"You were in shock, babe. It wasn't your fault. You probably would have died too if you had been in the house."

"Had I been in the house, the intruder wouldn't have stolen my jewellery or taken the car and there wouldn't have been a tragedy. Charlie, what did I do?"

Charlie tried to console Myra. He spoke of all the 'what-ifs' that were sheer speculation. He asked himself the same questions. What if he had returned home with Myra and the baby? What if he'd gone looking for her rather than just giving up? When the police said she didn't want contact?

"The what-ifs don't matter now. We're together and we will get through this together," he said, clinging to her.

Myra stopped crying and looked at Charlie.

"How long can we be together, Charlie? You've moved on without me," she said, pained.

"You didn't leave me too many choices," he replied.

"Am I too late?" she asked.

Charlie didn't respond. What was he going to say to this distraught woman? He felt more torn than ever between the past and the future.

Charlie took Myra out of the garden and over to the entertaining area to take a seat. He wondered how much Ruby had witnessed of the embrace and was relieved to see she was nowhere in sight. Settling Myra in the shade on a comfortable seat, he went inside to find some tissues and get them a drink.

"Everything okay?" asked Ruby.

"Yeah," Charlie replied. "Myra just had a bit of a breakdown, but she's okay."

"And how are you?"

"I'm okay, too. Just getting us a drink. Join us, won't you?" he said, without looking and disappearing back to Myra.

I'm okay, too, thanks for asking. No, I'm fine. I don't need a drink. Ruby's discomfort grew.

Outside, Myra had again composed herself as Charlie arrived with drinks. Eventually Charlie broached the subject of what her plans were. Was she staying in The Valley or not? As always, she remained aloof and non-committal. They continued talking well into the evening while Ruby waited in the background, acting as hostess rather than joining into conversations clearly didn't involve her. Myra reminisced about everything from their first meeting and university days to their wedding. Sensing this made Ruby uncomfortable, Charlie would change the subject to something less exclusive. However, Myra seemed only to be interested in reliving the past.

At ten o'clock, Ruby excused herself, saying she needed to sleep, leaving Charlie and his wife to have a final nightcap on the back deck.

"You always wanted to build the house down here," said Myra, smiling.

"Yeah, and I stand by it being the best spot on the block!" he said, laughing.

"Well, sitting here with you now, on a beautiful warm evening, I'd have to agree with you," said Myra, turning to Charlie and taking his hand. "Thank you, Charlie, for tonight, for bringing me back to face everything, for sharing the garden with me."

"Thank you for coming. I've missed you," he said spontaneously.

"Same."

Inside the bedroom, Ruby heard all they said through the open window. She hadn't wanted to eavesdrop, but the night was too warm for closed windows. As tears fell on the pillow, Ruby couldn't help but hear the father of her child tell another woman what she longed to hear.

¥

Myra left soon after. While Charlie walked Myra to her car, Ruby could no longer hear what they were saying. She did, however, time how long it took him to say goodbye to his former wife. She listened to his laugh bellow out through the night before hearing the start of the car engine.

Charlie remained outside for a little longer after Myra had gone before returning to the house. He stuck his head in the bedroom door, where Ruby pretended to be asleep. Closing the door, he went to the living room and turned on the television.

During the night, Ruby checked on Charlie and found him asleep on the couch with half a dozen empty beer bottles nearby.

The next morning, Ruby awoke, surprised the baby had slept for so long. She got up to check on her, only to find Charlie sitting with the baby in his arms. He whispered to his daughter, who lay in his arms with eyes wide, examining his face. Charlie looked up as Ruby entered the room.

"I didn't think she was hungry, so thought I'd let you sleep," he said simply.

"Thanks," said Ruby before heading for the kitchen to put the kettle on.

"You okay?" he called after her.

"Yep. Fine. You?"

"Ouch! Mummy's not happy," he said to Zoe.

Ruby ignored the comment. Making herself a cuppa, she returned to the lounge.

"Talk to me," he said. "What's going on?"

"You tell me, Charlie."

Charlie didn't respond and continued to play with his daughter's fingers.

"Do you want her back?"

Charlie looked up, surprised.

"I heard you. You can hear everything on the back deck when the bedroom window's open, remember?"

"What do you think you heard?" he asked defensively.

"Charlie, I'm tired. I don't want to do this. As you've said, you've got a lot of shit to sort through–with your wife. I think, for my sake, not yours, I'm going to stay with my sister for a while."

"When?"

"I don't know, this afternoon, I guess."

"When will you be back?"

Ruby looked at Charlie before replying, "I don't know."

"What? You're taking our daughter and just leaving?"

"Not 'just', Charlie. I've tried to be supportive. I welcomed your wife into my home and felt like I was the intruder. What was that comment of hers about hoping nothing happens to this one? Trying to tell me there's no room in your life for me and Zoe? I ... I'm done. I heard you say you've missed her. I saw the way you two held each other in the garden. I can't compete, Charlie, and I won't. If you decide you want the woman that has stood by you for the last few years, put up with some pretty selfish crap too, I might add, and the daughter that is alive, you know where to find me. But until you decide, I don't want to hear from you or see you."

Ruby rose to pack when Charlie called. "What about Zoe? Am I not allowed to see Zoe? You can't take my daughter away from me."

"Wow. Not even an 'I don't want you to go'?"

Chapter Twenty Four

Within two hours, Ruby had gone. Once again, Charlie sat alone with Toby on the back deck of the house. He sat reflecting on the choices he had made and was still continuing to make that seemed to keep being his undoing. What did he want? Who did he want?

He was deep in thought when he heard a car arriving. Charlie leapt up, hopeful that Ruby had changed her mind. Instead, he saw Myra. He'd forgotten he'd invited her back today and that they were going again to the cemetery to plant a new shrub on Issie's grave.

Myra got out of the car, all smiles, with a small *erica carnea* plant in her hand.

"Pirbright Rose," she called. "Flowers most of the year, apparently. It's a ground cover with gorgeous little apricot and purple-coloured flowers."

Charlie nodded.

"What's wrong?" she asked.

"Ruby's gone."

"What do you mean she's gone? Gone where?"

"Gone to stay with her sister."

"Oh," replied Myra with little emotion. "I'm supposed to say I'm sorry, but I'm not Charlie. I thought this was going to be just you and me. I ... she was our daughter."

"Gees, you really are heartless bitch sometimes."

"Charlie!"

He hastened to enter the house, followed closely by Myra.

"Charlie! Stop!"

"Do you have any compassion in your body?"

"I do, Charlie, and I am sorry. But it was a matter of time, really."

"What?" Charlie asked, perplexed.

Myra put the small plant on the kitchen bench before moving to Charlie's side.

"Charlie, I never stopped loving you and don't think you have me. Am I right?"

"But you don't need to be so heartless about what I've put that woman through. She's been a rock for me for the last few years. She's supported me, indulged me; you said it yourself. I've been a selfish prick and I top it off by bringing my wife into her home and expect her to welcome you with open arms."

"What do you want me to say, Charlie? I love you. I thought–last night you said you missed me. I thought we were going to try to–you know. Finish healing together and maybe try again."

Charlie walked away from Myra.

"Do you love me, Charlie?"

"Honestly? I don't know."

"Right, I see. I know you're confused, Charlie, but look at me," she said, standing beside him. "We were good together. This place–this block–has too many ghosts, Charlie. But we could make us work again."

"And what will I be, Myra? I'm assuming you're talking about moving to the city where I have no place. I'll just be another of your accessories."

"We don't have to move to the city. We can find some middle ground; always managed in the past! Didn't we? Charlie, we're good together. You know it and I know it. And if we're together, we will continue to be a real family for Issie G. Don't we owe it to her?"

"A real family. A real family doesn't run away when things get tough. A real family supports each other. A real family loves the good and the bad."

"We've been over this. I made a mistake. A very big one, I know that. But I love you. Please, don't turn your back on me."

"I let her go. I let her walk out that door with my daughter and didn't stop her. What was I thinking?"

"Do you love her, Charlie?"

"Yes, I do," he said, facing Myra. "Not like I loved you. It's different. But I do love her. And I feel like a right prick."

"You said 'loved'—past tense."

"I will always love you, Myra—"

"Then let's try again! For all our sakes."

"What room can you make for Zoe in this life together? And what was that coment yesterday about *hoping nothing happens to her*?"

"In time, I'm sure ... it's not easy, Charlie. I lost my daughter, remember? Having your replacement daughter will take some time to get used to. Babies trigger me. But, she will always be welcome in our home, visit on the holidays ..."

"In the holidays? Myra, I'm not losing a second daughter. I want to be her father! Not the man she visits in the holidays."

"I'm sorry, I didn't mean it like that," said Myra. "Maybe I should go. We can plant this another time."

"Yeah, that might be a good idea."

Charlie stood ridged not looking at Myra as she reached up to kiss him on the cheek before turning to leave. As she reached the passage, she stopped. "I love you, Charlie. Listen to your heart. It will tell you what to do," she said before leaving.

Beside him, Toby, seeming to sense his master's tension and nudged Charlie's leg. Charlie looked down and the trusty kelpie whined.

"Come on, mate," he said to Toby, heading for the sliding doors that lead to the entertainment area. They walked outside and could see Myra driving away. Charlie and Toby headed for the bush. Crossing the river on the fallen tree trunk, they began following the old track through the trees. Charlie always did his best thinking surrounded by towering gum trees that had stood there for hundreds of years. He always felt wisdom and strength surrounded him when he walked amongst these giants of the past. They struggled but managed to survive as he wished he could.

All he'd ever wanted was a wife, a house he could call home, and children to fill it. Was that too much to ask for, he wondered. He contemplated this thought and many more as he wandered through the scrub. Toby, seeming to have forgotten his troubled master, darted in and out of the scrub chasing lizards, bouncing on fallen leaves and bringing sticks of various sizes back to Charlie.

Once again, he found himself at the murky swimming hole. Sitting on his favourite boulder, he threw a stick repeatedly for Toby to retrieve. Eventually, Toby became tired and plonked at Charlie's feet, panting and looking hot.

"Jump in the water, mate. That'll cool you off," said Charlie.

Toby looked to where Charlie was pointing and back at Charlie, not understanding. Charlie stood and moved closer to the edge.

"In," he commanded, gesturing to the water. "Come on, Tobes, jump in! Come on!"

Toby wagged his tail energetically, looking from the water and back to Charlie. He faltered at the edge; unconvinced jumping in the water was a good idea. Toby barked at Charlie and danced around his feet.

"Come on, mate. I will if you do!" Charlie said.

Charlie moved closer to Toby to grab and throw him in, but Toby was too quick. He knew what Charlie was planning and got out of the way quickly, continuing to bark at his master. Charlie made another attempt, but Toby dodged out of the way again. Charlie feigned disinterest as Toby carefully moved back towards his master. For the final time, Charlie tried to get hold of Toby, but Toby was able to dodge him once more. However, Charlie managed to trip himself up and ended in the shallows of the water. Toby jumped in the shallow water after Charlie and they splashed and wrestled around the edges for a short time until Charlie got a mouth full of water.

For a moment he had forgotten the troubles he carried. But finding himself sitting in a pool of stagnant the water brought him back. He got out of the cesspool and called Toby with him.

Wet and dirty from the water, they made their way back toward the house. Tired from all the exercise, this time Toby walked down the track by his master's side. The track wasn't wide and often not big enough to walk side by side. So, Toby took the lead, almost protectively leading his master home.

Back at the house, Charlie got the hose out to wash the dirt and filth off the dog before cleaning himself up. Toby stood obediently for Charlie.

"I've gone and stuffed it up, mate," said Charlie, soaping up the dog. "Wanna swap places? You sort out the women. I'll sit in the sun lickin' my balls for a while. What do you say, hey? Sound good to you? Sounds good to me."

He turned, hearing footsteps approaching. So absorbed in his own little world, he hadn't noticed the tail of a car sitting in the driveway. Walking toward him was Billy.

"Mate, if you've come to give me a bollocking, don't bother. You can't say anything I haven't already said to myself."

"What the fuck, Charlie? What are you doing?'

"Word travels fast."

Charlie finished washing down the dog before Billy turned the hose on him.

"Oi!" Charlie yelled. "Easy, mate. I'll shower inside, if you don't mind."

Billy kept the hose on his brother, tightening the nozzle so the water pressure increased.

"Bill, cut it out. It hurts," Charlie yelled.

"Good!" replied Billy. "Maybe it'll bring you to your senses."

Charlie took his clothes off before entering the house by the back door. Once he showered and was clean again, he joined Billy on the back deck with a couple of beers.

“I don’t want to lose her,” he began. “If we can get through this, we can get through anything.”

Billy sat motionless, waiting for his brother to continue.

“She’s everything I want. Strong, independent, won’t take crap from me,” he said, laughing. “She’s a good mum and I’m a selfish prick.”

“Yeah, you are,” said Billy. “I’m assuming you’re talking about Myra.”

“No! I’m talking about Ruby! I got confused, okay? Myra came back, told me her side of the story and I felt compassion for her—just like you said I would. She’s been through hell, too. I see that now. But she didn’t love or trust me enough to turn to me when the shit hit the fan. She ran away.”

“But you still love her.”

“I always will, mate, but sometimes that’s not enough, is it?”

“What are you going to do?”

“Gonna see if I can convince Ruby to come home. If she doesn’t, I will be the biggest loser ever! Let my second chance just walk out that front door. No, I want her here. I want them here with me. Staying here, on this block, surviving the accident was one of the hardest things I’ve ever done. I’m not going to go through what I have just to chuck it all in and walk away with Myra. She’s a city girl, always was, always will be. My place is here.”

“Then you better get your shit together real quick. Finish what you need to with Myra and go get Ruby back, you daft twat.”

¥

The next day, Charlie called Myra to meet. She offered to come to the block, but Charlie suggested they meet by the river near the café in Warburton, where they met just a few short weeks back. As with their last meeting, Charlie arrived first. Leaning against the bonnet of the car, watching three young kids feeding and chasing the ducks. He couldn't actually remember a time when Myra was ready before him or early for anything.

She pulled up next to him as looked at his watch and smiled. She smiled back before asking, "What are you smiling at?"

"I was just thinking. I can't remember you ever being on time or early for anything." He looked at his watch again. "Ten minutes later, right on Myra-time."

She laughed and apologised for being so predictable. As she leaned in to give him a kiss, Charlie pulled back.

"Oh, sorry. Too public here?" she asked.

"No, it's not that, My," he said.

"Oh, I see." Myra sighed and turned to watch the river and the children opposite, them. Charlie delicately took her by the arm and led her toward a picnic table to sit.

"I love you, Myra. Always have, always will."

"But–" she said.

"I can't go backward now."

"Backwards? Wow, don't hold back, Charlie."

"Hear me out. I needed you, Myra. You hurt me like I've never been hurt before. Okay, I made mistakes, which led to you not feeling you could turn to me. But you let me think you were dead. I was this close to being arrested for manslaughter! And you would have let me go to jail."

"Charlie, I was dealing with depression. I wasn't functioning properly. I didn't know."

"It just highlights what different people we are."

"What about what you said last night, that you missed me? Did you mean it?"

"Yes. I have missed you, but that's not enough to go back."

"You keep saying 'go back'. I don't want to go back either, Charlie. I want a fresh start. With you."

"In the city–sorry, okay, you said you'd compromise on location as long as it's not here," he said as she protested. "My business is here. My life is here. My daughters are here. I can't leave them or my life here, Myra. I don't want to."

"Well," began Myra. "I'm glad my return has brought healing for you." A wan smile crossed her face. Charlie's heart was breaking for her.

"I'm sorry, My."

"And I'm assuming this plan to stay near your business and daughters includes the new lady?"

"Ruby. Her name is Ruby. And yes, if it's not too late. If I haven't completely blown it with her."

"You're a good man, Charlie. You always were. She'd be silly not to take you back."

Myra, realising that her relationship had forever changed with Charlie, thought about the other reasons she'd returned. She still had loose ends to tie up before she could leave. She didn't know how long it would take. Maybe a month, maybe two.

"Charlie," she began sadly, "I ... I'm not ... augh!"

"What? Healed?"

"I can't just walk away yet."

"Then don't. Stay as long as you need to. I'm not turning my back on you, Myra. I will be there for you through this. I'm just not coming with you when you go. I have to put Ruby first for a change."

"Would you consider coming to counselling with me?"

Charlie took a sharp breath in.

"Not marriage counselling," she quickly added. "Trauma counselling. It would help me, Charlie, if you would come with me. You're the only person in the world–"

"I know. I know," he said sadly. "Yeah, I'll come with you. Not sure how Ruby's gonna take it, but I'll come."

"I'll talk to her if you like," Myra offered.

"Oh no. I don't think I want you near her again after last time!"

"What are you talking about?"

Charlie again brought up the insensitive comment she'd made to the brand-new mother about hoping nothing happened to her daughter. Myra winced and apologised. She admitted to being a bitch at that moment and resented Ruby being able to give you the second chance she longed to give him.

"It will come, Myra, just ... deal with the old shit before creating new shit. That's my advice–speaking from experience."

Myra laughed and leaned her head against Charlie's shoulder. Charlie put his arm around her and gave her an affectionate hug, which, to Myra, felt like her brother had just hugged her. She'd lost him for the future but would savour the moments she had with him.

¥

Ruby had said she wanted no contact with Charlie until he'd worked out what he wanted. He'd done that, quicker than he'd expected, too. Charlie deemed it an opportune moment to call and express his love and longing for her, Zoe, and their return home. However, Ruby wasn't so ready. She asked if Myra would continue to be in his life and when he said he'd agreed to see a counsellor with her, Ruby hung up the phone. Charlie called repeatedly, but Ruby refused to pick up the phone. After the tenth consecutive attempt, he received a text message.

"Stop ringing, Charlie. Like I said, finish dealing with the past before contacting me. I can't go through it and don't want to. Adjusting to the baby is more than I can cope with. I will not torture myself watching you go to counselling with your wife. Go do what you need to and leave me alone until it's over–if it ever will be over. If you want to see Zoe, we can work something out through Col. *I don't* want to see or hear from you."

While it pained him greatly, Charlie would accept her wishes. Charlie planned for the future with a new purpose in his sight. To win back the woman with whom he wanted to grow old. As he had promised, he wouldn't walk away from Myra, but he wouldn't allow her to be the leading lady in his life any longer.

Chapter Twenty Five

While Myra had been in no hurry to begin the counselling sessions, Charlie had pushed for it. Insisting too much time had been lost already since the incident. The sessions needed to start immediately and be twice a week if she was serious about wanting closure and healing and not just playing a game.

Myra protested, saying closure couldn't be forced or hurried. It would take as long as it would take. While Charlie agreed, he also made it clear that his attendance at these sessions was not infinite. He would attend to give them closure in their relationship and deal with as much of the event that affected him. But she was the only one who could deal with the grief and regret she carried. He couldn't be a part of that.

And so, the sessions began. Twice a week, Myra and Charlie went to Dr. Silvers discussing their loss and plans to move forward.

Charlie also made plans for his future with Ruby. Against her wishes, he sent her the occasional message of love, telling her what he was doing around the block. He erected a childproof fence on the back deck so that, when she was older, Zoe could play without danger near the river. He also constructed a fence of sorts from the entertainment area to Issie's Garden so that Zoe could play outside safely. He finally updated the nursery with the growth chart and children's frieze that Ruby had bought months ago to put on the wall.

Charlie would drive to the peninsula to visit his daughter as often as possible. It made no difference to him who picked up Zoe and met him at the local park as long as he saw her every chance he could. The three-and-a-half-hour return drive was a small price to pay for precious minutes with his daughter.

All the while, Ruby remained true to her word. He heard nothing from her, and Col and the sister were always reluctant to divulge anything. Charlie didn't blame them or Ruby. He needed to prove himself; he understood and respected that, even though he didn't find it easy. Many a night, he'd lay in the empty bed and feel like he was again talking to ghosts. He didn't know what he'd do if she didn't return.

The only thing he was sure of, he was finally leaving the past behind. If Ruby didn't return, he'd be heartbroken. But he couldn't change her decision or entice her back. Reluctantly, he would accept her decision.

The days grew shorter and nights cooler as autumn moved toward winter. The counselling sessions with Dr. Silvers had ceased for Charlie as Myra continued to work through her loss and adjust to the future without her husband and baby daughter.

Having drawn the line in the sand with Myra, Charlie returned home from work one evening to find Myra sitting in her car in the driveway waiting for him. He braced himself as he approached her.

"Myra, this is unexpected. Everything alright?" he asked apprehensively.

"Yes," she said, smiling up at him. "Just wondered if you'd have dinner with me."

Charlie stiffened.

"Don't worry! I'm not going to seduce you or anything. It's just, I think I'll be leaving soon and would like to say a proper goodbye."

"When are you going?" he asked.

"Not completely sure yet. I think I've still got a few more sessions with Dr Silvers, but then heading back toward civilisation," she said with a cheeky grin.

"When did you want to have dinner?"

"Tonight?" she replied sheepishly.

"Tonight! Okay, come in," he said. "I'd like to change and freshen up a bit if that's okay. Have anywhere in mind?"

"I was hoping you could suggest some place. New beginnings and all I thought somewhere we have no history."

They entered the house and Toby greeted his master with a display of bouncing affection. As Toby bounced toward Myra, she instinctively pulled back. While she liked dogs, she preferred them at a distance and certainly not in the house.

"You going to let him in the house when Zoe returns?" she asked.

"He's family! Of course," replied Charlie with a laugh, much to Myra's disgust.

It didn't take Charlie long to shower, change, and be ready for dinner. Not knowing where to go that they had no history, they jumped online to look for somewhere tucked away that they hadn't tried before. As Charlie's computer came on, a photo of Ruby and Zoe on the day she was born appeared as his backdrop.

"Hello, ladies," he said blindly. Then, remembering Myra was standing behind him, he turned and apologised. "I always say hello to them when I start the computer. Sorry. Habit."

"Don't apologise. I'm happy for you, Charlie. Really, I am. It's a cute photo. And she seems nice."

"Who have you been speaking with?"

"Charlie, this is the country. Everybody has their noses in everyone's business. I haven't talked to anyone, but others have been more than happy to tell me how wonderful she is!"

"Oh, Gees. Sorry."

"Don't be. It was hard initially, but then Dr Silvers helped me sort through it. It's okay. I'm okay with you being in love with another woman. And I think I'm ready to fall in love again, too. Didn't expect to be saying that six months ago," she said with a laugh.

"No, it's been a big few months," said Charlie absently, as he searched for a place to eat. "We're going to have to travel."

"Thought we might."

"What about that place in Lilydale you always wanted to go to?" Charlie asked.

"History."

"History? How? We never went there."

"But we thought about it."

"Gees, woman. Okay," he said, turning back to the computer. "Here. Does this count as history?" he asked, pointing out an old hotel.

"We've been there!"

"Yes, but it shut down for a few years and only recently reopened under new management. Technically–"

"No! Keep looking."

"Okay. Got it. Anda's Kitchen in Seville."

"I don't know that one."

"Ah ha! Perfect. Neither do I. Let's go!"

They jumped in separate cars so that Myra could go straight home after the meal and drove the thirty-five-minute drive to Seville and the chosen restaurant, only to find it closed. Charlie put the only two options he could think of on the table: Wandin Fish and Chips or Dave's Pizza and Pasta. Myra decided on Dave's, as it sounded marginally more classy.

"I haven't been completely honest with you, Charlie, but I thought getting you a public place, you may take it a little more kindly than anywhere else," Myra said as she went for another piece of pizza.

Charlie froze, waiting for her to continue.

"There is one last thing I'd like us to do together before I leave."

"What's that?" Charlie asked uneasily.

"We still haven't planted the erica at the cemetery. Issie's birthday is coming up in a few weeks and I thought, if you'd be open to it, we could plant it on her birthday."

"I don't know Myra. I like the gesture and all, but I'm pretty keen on Ruby and Zoe returning home as soon as possible. She won't talk to me, let alone come home if I'm still having contact with you."

"Let me talk to her."

"No! I've told you before. That's not gonna happen."

"Charlie, please. This will be the final closure for me and that part of my life. Don't ... look like that. Issie will always be a part of me and I will return to see her. I just want us to do one last thing for her together as her parents. Please, Charlie. Will you think about it, at least? You don't need to decide now."

"I'll think about it," he replied.

Charlie and Myra went their separate ways at the end of the evening and, for the first time in a while, Charlie felt the most awful time of his life was coming to an end. Myra was preparing to leave and he was alright with that. He would contact Ruby soon and hoped she'd start thinking of returning.

The next day, Charlie tried to call Ruby and, as usual, she didn't pick up the phone. He messaged her but got no reply. He rang Col, who refused to get involved. He rang her sister, Claire, but she, too, didn't reply. Out of desperation, Charlie jumped in his car to begin the long drive to where Ruby was living.

The winter day was typical: dark, gloomy and wet. As he drove, he messaged clients cancelling appointments, saying he had to handle some urgent family matters. He'd come too far and lost too much to not give it everything he had to win back Ruby. He wouldn't make the same mistakes twice.

The weather made travel slower than he'd hoped. Or was it just his anxious mind playing tricks on him? He endeavoured to reassure himself that there was no urgency as they had a lifetime together, but it offered little solace. The whole way down the peninsula, he rehearsed what he would say. She's leaving soon, come home. I love you, come home. I don't want to be without you and Zoe, he thought. I don't want to be without you! All he could do was try.

Charlie arrived at Ruby's sister's house mid-afternoon only to find a few cars in the driveway, suggesting they had visitors. Charlie hadn't expected to deal with other people. In his little fantasy, he was coming to sweep Ruby off her feet and convince her to come home with him. He sat in the car briefly, thinking about what he should do. He definitely wasn't about to leave again without seeing her but did not know how long the visitors would be there.

As he sat in the car, he looked at one of the visiting cars. A prickle of recognition stirred him. He knew that car, but whose was it? Myra. He realised it was the same as Myra's car. He berated himself for his foolishness; the vehicle was identical to Myra's, but not necessarily hers. Why would Myra be here and how would she know where Ruby was, he pondered.

Two minutes later, however, his worst nightmare came true. Myra walked out the door, closely followed by Ruby and the baby. He sat stunned for a second before pulling himself together enough to get out of the car. He watched as Myra shook Ruby's hand and turned to walk away.

Charlie crossed the street towards the women. Ruby was the first to see him but said nothing.

"Charlie," said Myra. "We weren't expecting you."

"I could say the same, Myra. What are you doing here?"

"I came to talk to Ruby," she explained nonchalantly as Ruby remained silent. "I'm sorry, I have to go. Got a plane to catch. But I'll be back next week. Think about what I said, Ruby," said Myra, taking her leave.

Charlie turned to look at Ruby, waiting for an explanation. Ruby said little other than, "Come inside."

Charlie followed Ruby into the living room and offered Charlie a seat before handing Zoe over to her father. Charlie, distracted, took the baby but kept his gaze on Ruby.

"Can I get you anything?" Ruby offered.

"Ruby, what was that about?"

"Trust me, I've been asking myself the same thing for the last hour."

"I didn't give her the address," said Charlie.

"I know. One downside of living in a small community, someone else did. She wouldn't say who, but my guess is Mrs Cronin."

"What did she want?"

"Well," Ruby began. "She came to tell me what a wonderful man you are and how much you love me."

Charlie cringed.

"Oh, wait, there's more."

"Okay."

"She informed me she was leaving The Valley permanently. Her mission was to make peace with you and the ghosts of the past, and she completed that. She's going back to the city with the closure she needs. Life has never looked or felt so positive for her! Isn't that wonderful, Charlie? While I've spent month after month in hell because of that woman, she came to tell me how glorious life is now!"

"Ruby, I'm so–"

"Don't you dare! Keep your apologies to yourself. Don't you dare tell me you'll make it up to me. It's been hard enough keeping away from you, but to have her come here to see me and tell me I can have you back? That was the icing on the cake, Charlie."

"Is that what she said?"

"Not in so many words, but basically."

"I think you're mistaken, Rubes."

"Oh, of course you do. Side with the wife over me–yet again!"

"No, no, Ruby," said Charlie, putting the baby on the play mat and going to Ruby's side. He held her at arm's length, afraid of fully embracing her.

“Ruby, we had dinner last night and Myra said–”

“You had dinner with her? Oh, this just keeps getting better,” said Ruby, pulling away from him.

“Ruby, stop it!” he yelled. “I’m all for you giving me a hard time about my behaviour, how I’ve neglected you. But things have changed, and you need to hear it. If you still want to be angry with me, then ... then there’s not much I can do about it. But at least be angry with me for the right reasons. You said you wouldn't come home until I'd resolved things with Myra. I've done that. Now the ball's in your court. Either you listen or it's over.”

Ruby stood where she was with her back him. Charlie was grateful she didn't leave the room. He continued quickly.

“Ruby, I’ve been a fool, but I kind of had to be. Remember when we first got together, I said I had a lotta stuff to work through? Well, it’s taken the best part of three months to do that, but I’ve worked through it. Myra is my ex-wife–or will be soon enough. What we went through and experienced, no one should ever have to go through. And I’m really sorry that you had to go through it, too. Whether or not you can see a future for us, I won’t be going back to Myra. Too much has happened. I’ve moved on. I love you, Ruby, and I want you by my side. You’ve proven yourself to be more of a support than any man could ever ask in a partner. Please, Ruby, come home. Myra will be gone soon enough. I miss you,” he said, moving closer to stand by her and gently place his hands on her arms again.

“She asked me to come with you to plant the erica on Isabella’s birthday.”

“She did?” he said, surprised. “What did you say?”

“I’d think about it.”

“Ruby, see. There is no me and Myra anymore. She knows you’re the one I love. You are my future. She’s the past. I won't plant the shrub with Myra unless you're beside me. Issie is Zoe’s sister, remember.”

“You hurt me, Charlie.”

"I know I did. And it will take me a lifetime to make up for it. But let me try."

Ruby turned toward Charlie and eased into his arms as he wiped the tears from her eyes. They stood holding each other for some time, not saying anything. Eventually, baby Zoe interrupted her parents with a cry for attention. The two parted, and Charlie smiled at her.

"Issie's sister, hey?"

"Of course."

"It's gonna take me some time, Charlie."

"You take all the time you need as long as you return. You and Zoe are a part of my past and the only future I want."

¥

Two weeks later, Ruby and Zoe returned home to Gilderoy. Charlie anad Ruby had talked for hours each day about the future, about the weather, football and local gossip. When Ruby eventually returned, Charlie had done all the minor jobs he'd promised to do one day, to Ruby's delight.

¥

Isabella's sixth birthday arrived and Charlie bundled Ruby and Zoe into the car on the cold winter's day for the drive to the cemetery, where they would meet Myra. A light drizzle fell as they pulled up and, to Charlie's surprise, Myra stood under a large tree, waiting for him.

"You go, Charlie," said Ruby. "Issie is your daughter. I'll wait in the car with Zoe."

Charlie hesitantly got out and went to Myra under the tree. Several glances back at the car told Ruby they were talking about her. Suddenly, Myra came toward the car. Ruby lowered the window.

"Come on. Zoe has a right to wish her sister a happy birthday even if... well, she's too young to know what a birthday is and Issie's...you know. Please, Ruby. Come."

The strange little family comprising of Charlie, his soon-to-be ex-wife and mother to his first daughter, his partner and newest daughter stood in the miserable drizzling rain to plant the small bush.

www.ingramcontent.com/pod-product-compliance
Lightning Source LLC
LaVergne TN
LVHW090946080826
845145LV00003B/908

* 9 7 8 0 6 4 5 3 7 7 0 5 7 *